When Ratboy Lived Next Door

Chris Woodworth

When Ratboy
Lived Next Door

Farrar, Straus and Giroux
New York

Copyright © 2005 by Christina Woodworth
All rights reserved
Distributed in Canada by Douglas & McIntyre Publishing Group
Printed in the United States of America
Designed by Barbara Grzeslo
First edition, 2005
10 9 8 7 6 5

www.fsgkidsbooks.com

Library of Congress Cataloging-in-Publication Data
Woodworth, Chris, date.
    When Ratboy lived next door / Chris Woodworth.— 1st ed.
        p.   cm.
    Summary: When his strange family moves into her quiet south Indiana
town, sixth-grader Lydia Carson initially despises her new neighbor and
classmate, who seems as wild as the raccoon that is his closest companion.
    ISBN-13: 978-0-374-34677-5
    ISBN-10: 0-374-34677-1
    [1. Raccoons as pets—Fiction.   2. Neighbors—Fiction.   3. Brothers and
sisters—Fiction.   4. Family problems—Fiction.   5. Alcoholism—Fiction.
6. Indiana—History—20th century—Fiction.]   I. Title.

PZ7.W8794 Wh 2005
[Fic]—dc22
                                                      2004050634

To my dad, Richard Lincicum,
for instilling in me his love of books,
and to my mom, Francee Lincicum,
for swallowing her fear and letting me ride my bike
across a busy road to visit the library all by myself

When Ratboy Lived Next Door

1

May 18, 1962

The sweet ring of the school bell echoed through the building at exactly 3:00 p.m., and we were free of school—at least for the weekend. In two more weeks, we'd be free for the whole summer.

I lifted my desk lid and grabbed my books. Before the lid banged down, I threw myself into the swarm of other sweaty sixth graders bottlenecked at the door. Mrs. Warren was mouthing her usual "Class-don't-push! Class-don't-rush! Class-don't-*don't*!"

It was the same speech we got every day at 3:00, but you could tell her heart wasn't in it anymore. Even Mrs. Warren must have sensed that summer had both arms stretched out, beckoning us to leave our schoolbooks and number-two pencils behind.

Outside, I yanked the back of my skirt up between my legs and pushed it through my belt so it wouldn't get caught in the bike chain. Then I threw my books into the basket on my candy red Schwinn and gave the kickstand a good swat with my foot. I started pedaling straight toward chubby Bobby Wayans. He stood in the center of the road, wearing the bright yellow crossing-guard band across his chest.

"Stop!" Bobby yelled at me, holding his sign high in the air. "I said *stop*!"

I didn't even slow down.

"Lydia Carson, I'll get you into trouble for this!" he shouted, butt-kissing teacher's pet that he was.

"Well, Bobby, you can always *try*!" I hollered back.

I hadn't liked Bobby for three years, ever since he told on me for putting a toad on the refreshment table during Vacation Bible School. Everybody else thought it was funny, but not Bobby. He was probably afraid the toad would eat a brownie and that would mean one less brownie for him. From the day he became the school crossing guard, I made it my mission to never stop when he told me to.

I swerved just before I reached him. Then I tightened my grip on the handlebars and slammed on the brakes. I spun my bike in a circle and hightailed it out of there before someone with real authority saw me.

I rode through town toward my daddy's filling station. I always went there to do my homework when the weather was good, even on Friday afternoons. The wind blew the short waves of dark hair away from my smiling face. As soon as school was out for the summer, I could pack up these sorry school dresses and ride away from Maywood Grade School for the last time. Next year I would be a seventh grader over at Maywood Junior-Senior High.

The only bad thing about summer coming was that I probably wouldn't see my very best friend, Rae Anne. Her daddy farmed land as far away from Maywood as you could get and still be in our school district. She had a long bus ride to and from school.

Her grandma, Mrs. Ogle, used to live next door to me. In the summers, Rae Anne spent as much time there as she could, and I was at Mrs. Ogle's house more than my own. Rae Anne and I were so much alike we were almost twins.

After Mr. Ogle died last year, Mrs. Ogle went to live with Rae Anne and her family. Now the house was empty and Rae Anne wouldn't be visiting. Her folks didn't mind bringing her to visit her grandma, but they'd never make the trip just so she could play with a friend.

I was coming up to the post office. It was a small building with a flagpole whose cord snapped so on a windy day it would scare the daylights out of you if you weren't expecting it. Everyone had a post office box there. The government wasn't going to spend good money on a letter carrier for a town the size of Maywood, Indiana.

As I rode past, I swung to the right to tap the flagpole with my left hand. I don't know who started tapping the flagpole, but all the kids did it. It was just something you did, same as breathing.

I picked up my pace at the office of the *Maywood Press*. It was my mother's newspaper. She took over as its publisher when she moved to Maywood, before she met my daddy. The only week she didn't put out a paper was the week I was born. You'd think her office would be a good place to do homework, but whenever I went there Mother gave me an impatient "Yes, Lydia?" that said I'd better have a good excuse for stopping by. I got the feeling that needing a place to do homework didn't qualify, so I hardly ever went there. And I guess that was the way Mother wanted it because she never invited me.

I didn't stop until I came to the library. Nanna had asked

me to return her book, and she would never forgive me if I forgot and she had to pay a fine.

I parked my bike in front and released my skirt from my belt. My shoelace had come undone and I was bending over to tie it when I heard a clicking noise in the distance, kind of a cross between a motor running and a cat purring. I paused, still bent over, because it was such a strange noise that I was trying to figure out what it was. Suddenly I was pushed forward as something heavy landed on my back. Sharp spikes poked their way up my spine.

Acting on instinct and a fear so mighty I could have lifted a building, I reached up over my head, grabbed whatever it was, and hurled it away from me. At the same time, I lost my balance and stumbled forward against my bike. It went crashing down with me on top. I heard brakes squealing and looked up just in time to see that I'd thrown a raccoon into the side of an oncoming car.

A boy with reddish blond hair came running out of Hanson's A&P. He had a real worried look. I was just about to say that I was all right. I wasn't going to cry or act like a baby. I could take care of myself. But before I could say anything, he sped right past me. He dropped the Popsicle he'd been holding and picked up the raccoon, cooing to it as if it were a baby or something. At first it seemed dazed. Then it started tearing at him, trying to get out of his arms.

A man opened the door of the stopped car. "Oh no! Did I hit anybody?"

Then he took in the scene. "You mean it was just a coon?" He pulled out a bandanna and wiped his forehead. "Thank God!"

He came over to me and in one move pulled me up by my elbow and righted my bicycle. "I didn't hit you, did I, honey?"

"No, sir. I'm fine," I said, and I guess I was. My knees were just a little bloody. "I was nearly scared to death, that's all. That coon ran straight up my back!"

"Well, they're pretty slick creatures. He was probably rummaging around garbage cans. They're known for that," the man said and, reassured that he hadn't killed anybody, got in his car and took off.

I looked at the raccoon, now on the sidewalk, and saw a rope fashioned into a collar around its neck. Another rope was hanging from the collar like a leash, and the boy was holding it tight. His face was so white it made his freckles stand out like strawberries in cream. I saw something else on his face, too: pure hatred.

"He don't eat garbage. And you're lyin'—he wouldn't touch your skinny back with a ten-foot pole," he spat out. "He was tied up waitin' on me at the grocery store, you scrawny sack of bones." Then he took one hand off the coon long enough to push me. Hard. I stepped backward onto my own loose shoestring. I reached out to keep my balance, but it was no use. All I grabbed was air. For the second time that day, my bike and I went crashing to the ground—only now it was my rear end that got banged up.

I finally untangled myself and looked around. The boy and his raccoon were gone. Nobody else seemed to have noticed what happened, which was a good thing. It was bad enough to be bullied by some hick straight from the hills without anybody seeing it.

I gathered my homework and put it back into my basket.

Then I wiped the dust off the library book. Nanna would be fit to be tied if I ruined it. She wouldn't even let me set a book down on the return desk and walk out, the way everybody else did. I always had to hand it to Mrs. Green so that Nanna could rest assured it had been returned, safe and sound.

Nanna was my great-aunt and had raised me from a baby because Mother worked. Nanna's first name was Lydia. Daddy named me after her. I figured he borrowed Nanna's name just so he could call me *something*, since I had no name at all for the first three days of my life. I doubt Mother had an opinion one way or another, seeing as how I still didn't have a middle name. Nanna's full name was Lydia Gladys Baldwin. It sure wasn't pretty, but it was better than the name on my birth certificate: Lydia (none) Carson—as if I were nothing inside.

When I had made sure the book was okay, I slowly climbed the library steps. I opened the door and tried to walk quietly, each step echoing in the stillness. I wished for the hundredth time that Nanna would bring back her own dang books. There was something so somber about the place. I had decided long ago that happiness and excitement were feelings that had no business in a library or a church.

Even though the library had just one big room, I didn't see Mrs. Green right away.

"Oh, hello, Lydia! Be with you in a minute!"

I about jumped out of my skin as Mrs. Green fairly yelled from her perch on the ladder behind me. "Afternoon, Miz Green. That's fine," I whispered. Mrs. Green had just become our librarian and hadn't learned that shushing people, herself included, was part of the job.

She climbed down and said, "So, Lydia, are you checking

that book out or bringing it back?" She took Nanna's book from me. Then she saw my legs and called out louder than a librarian should, "My goodness! What happened to you?"

Before I could answer, she pulled my skirt back to see my knees. "Lydia Carson, you have blood just dripping down your legs! Were you in a bike wreck?"

"Well . . ."

"Never mind that for now. Sit in this chair while I get out my first aid kit." She pulled a chair out for me, its legs screeching across the floor.

I sat down and, sure enough, there was blood running down my legs. Just as she came back, I was scrunching my socks down so they wouldn't get wet.

"We'll have you fixed up in no time," Mrs. Green said while she rummaged through the box.

"Thank you kindly, Miz Green. I didn't know I was hurt that bad."

"I've been telling my husband that you kids would have a bike wreck, as fast as you come up that road. 'You just wait and see!' is what I told him."

"I didn't exactly have a bike wreck. I mean, I did fall into my bike. I got pushed is really more like it."

"Pushed! What do you mean, pushed?"

"It was the strangest thing. First a raccoon ran right up my back! I didn't know it was a raccoon, of course. I guess it wouldn't have mattered if I did. I threw it off me and it flew right into the side of a car."

Mrs. Green stopped working on my knees for a minute and said, "Lydia, I'm not angry with you about the bike wreck. You don't need to make up a story."

"No, ma'am! I promise it's the truth! And there was this boy, he owns the coon, I guess. He was so mad at me that he pushed me. Mad at *me* when his raccoon started all the trouble!"

"A boy! Why didn't you say so? Sounds to me like you have a beau, Lydia Carson," she said as she packed up her first aid kit.

"Beau? Oh, no, Miz Green," I said, standing up. "You've got it all wrong! I've never seen this boy before in my entire life!"

But Mrs. Green was finished with me. "Hello! How are you this fine day?" she said to a tiny old lady standing at the desk clutching some books. I started to leave.

"Oh, Lydia, don't run off yet! I need you to give your mother something. It will save me a trip to the newspaper," Mrs. Green said, looking through the papers on her desk.

"I have the titles of movies that will be shown next month. Your mother is going to print them in the paper. If I can just find them, that is."

She turned to the lady and said, "Isn't this exciting? Our little town will be showing its own movies! The first one is tonight, you know."

And she was off and running, telling the lady about the new Friday-night Free Shows. Mrs. Green's husband, Sam, had come up with the idea of having Maywood's merchants chip in to rent the movies. Sam's plan was to project them out of the library window onto the Laundromat wall next door. There was a nice, grassy lot in between where people would sit.

Folks would be drawn to the movies and then would shop in Maywood rather than drive the thirty miles to the bigger town of Aylesville. Sam owned Green's Appliance Store. Daddy told me it "like to killed" Sam every time he saw a delivery van from out of town bring new appliances to Maywood.

"Yessir, my Sam just walked right into that city council meeting and told them that Maywood was dying on the vine."

Clearly, the days of checking out a book without a twenty-minute conversation had vanished when Mrs. Green took the job. I wondered if the old woman had caught on.

"Sam told them, time was when all he had to do to draw a crowd on a Friday night was have a television set running in the window of his appliance store. Of course, these days most folks own a television. That's why he came up with the movie idea to keep Maywood's money in Maywood. Just like the good Lord intended. Ah, here's the list!"

"I'll give it to Mother, Miz Green."

"Thank you, Lydia! And you be careful out there. A person never knows what strange animal might attack!" she said in that hearty voice of hers.

"Yes, ma'am. I will." And, purely out of habit, I said goodbye very quietly to Mrs. Green.

My knees didn't want to bend too much with the big bandages she'd put on them, so I was grateful the road slanted enough to allow me to coast the rest of the way to Daddy's Sinclair filling station. The big green dinosaur on the sign was tall enough that you could see it over the top of the trains that ran on the tracks along the other side.

Daddy said the Sinclair people put up such a tall sign because they were afraid some traveler, impatient from waiting on a train to pass, would hurry through Maywood without knowing the Sinclair was there, and they'd miss a gas sale. If they missed every strange car traveling through Maywood in a year, that'd probably figure out to be about eight cars. Still and all, it made me feel mighty good to know the first thing anyone saw coming into town was the sign of my daddy's filling station.

Grabbing my books out of the basket, I limped inside and eased my sore rear into the black plastic chair that sat in the corner of the office. It was there for whoever stopped in to toss a few words back and forth with Daddy during the day. It was also there for anyone waiting on him to fix a flat. I always felt it was there just for me.

Daddy was singing "I Fall to Pieces" along with Patsy Cline on the radio and hadn't heard me come in, which was just as well. I wasn't sure I wanted to tell him about the boy and the raccoon. Daddy liked to give people "the benefit of the doubt," a saying I'd heard so much it made me want to scream. Just once I wished he'd say, "Come on. I'm going to give that boy a talking-to for hurting my daughter like that!" But no, Daddy would more than likely say, "Well, I'm sure he feels bad about it now, Lydia. That's punishment enough."

I decided to pull my skirt down over my bandaged knees and keep my mouth shut.

Daddy had a blue Buick on the hoist in the south bay. He was under it, letting oil drip from its pan, when he heard the buzzer that signaled a car had run over the snakelike plastic hose out by the pumps. He wiped his hands on a grease rag and tucked it into his back pocket. There's a grease rag stuck in the picture of every memory I have of Daddy at work.

He hurried out to help his new customer because he never

wanted a person to have to wait for service. You would have thought there was another place to get gas in Maywood.

When he came in, he acted surprised to find me sitting there. "Why, Ladybug! I was just wondering why the day suddenly seemed brighter. I should have known you were here."

Daddy always said things like that to me. It made me think he felt that he barely existed until I showed up. It was a nice change from Mother. However much space I took up around her seemed to be space she needed for something else.

Daddy walked over to the pop cooler and lifted the lid. He said the same thing he said every time I came: "Seems to me the Choc-ola isn't selling like it should. I need to get rid of a bottle. Think you could help me out?"

"I might." It was the same thing I said every time, too.

"How much homework you got today?"

"Too much! Same as usual."

Daddy chuckled. "That's too bad. I hoped you'd have time to run home and meet the new neighbors and their kids before supper."

I nearly choked on my drink. I'd been praying folks with kids would move in next door.

"Daddy! Really? How old are their kids? Do they have girls? Tell me they have girls, Daddy!"

"Why, Lydia, my head's about to explode with all these questions. I don't think I can answer so many. I guess I'd just better go back and finish Fritz's oil change until I can think clearer."

"Daddy!" I grabbed his arm before he could escape.

"Okay, okay. I'll tell you what I know." He laughed. "They stopped in here for gas on their way to the house, which is how

I found out. Their last name's Merrill and they have a girl, oh, about four years old, I'd say. They have a son a couple of years older than you and another son your age."

He looked proud as Punch. "Daddy, you're kidding, right? Tell me you're teasing."

The way his smile faded told me he wasn't. "Teasing about what?"

"Oh, Daddy, you mean to tell me the only girl is a little kid and the one my age is a *boy*?"

"Well, yeah, that's what I said." He looked confused and a little hurt that his big news wasn't so big after all.

I wasn't good at praying on a one-to-one basis. But ever since Rae Anne's grandma, Mrs. Ogle, had moved, I'd had plenty to pray about. On Sunday mornings, squashed in the pew between Daddy and Nanna, I had prayed hard and steady that a new girl my age would move into the neighborhood. I had been very specific about that.

I didn't care so much about the older boy. I'd stay out of his hair and I figured he'd stay outa mine. But to have a new neighbor my age who was a boy—and for the only girl to be a little kid! Well, I wouldn't be caught dead playing with either one.

I picked up my arithmetic book and sat back down. I didn't say it out loud, but I couldn't help thinking that for someone with a reputation for being almighty, God surely could make a mess of a good prayer.

Just when I thought things were as bad as they could get, Daddy said, "Hey, I know something that might cheer you. The neighbor boy who's your age? Well, you're not going to believe this, but he has a pet raccoon!"

2

I ran into the house, stopped, and out of habit poked my rear end out to catch the screen door before it slammed—a purely dumb move considering how tender my backside was. Then I headed straight for my bedroom to change clothes. Tonight was the first Free Show, *Saginaw Trail*, starring Gene Autry, and I couldn't wait.

Rae Anne had been trying to talk her folks into coming since we first heard about the shows. But a free movie didn't have the draw for them that it did for most folks. Living so far away, it was easier for them to do their shopping in Aylesville. Rae Anne said her mom and dad felt it was a pure waste of gas to drive into Maywood, but she was determined. The last time I saw Rae Anne determined was when she wanted to get her waist-length hair cut into a pixie. Her mama said, "Absolutely not." Rae Anne was too much of a good girl to take a whack at her own hair, as I might have. She just never combed it from that day on, and when her mama tried to brush it, Rae Anne would cry marble-sized tears. Finally her mother took her to Kathleen's Klip and Kurl in Aylesville and got her a pixie cut.

Since Rae Anne was determined again, I had every reason to believe she would be at the Free Show.

I carefully put the list of movies Mrs. Green had given me

into my pants pocket. I hurried back down the stairs, swung wide on the newel post, and jumped. I kept hoping I'd make it past the linen closet door. As usual, I landed a couple of inches short.

Just then, Mother and Daddy walked up to the front door. With downtown Maywood being only four blocks long, Daddy never drove to work. He always stopped by the newspaper and walked Mother home.

I made sure my shirt was tucked in, then took the movie list out of my pocket and smoothed it. Mother came in the door first.

"Hi, Mother! How are you today?"

"Tired."

"Oh, well, maybe you'll feel better when we get to the Free Show."

"Yes, the Free Show. Interviewing people, taking pictures—it sounds very restful," she said drily.

This wasn't going at all the way I'd planned. I tried again. "Um, Miz Green at the library asked me to give you this. It's the list of movies for the paper." I held it out to her.

She gave a big sigh, as if it were too much to think about. "Thank you, Lydia," she said and, without looking at it or me, laid it on the hall stand.

That feeling stole over me, the one that made me feel like a magnet turned the wrong way. The more I tried to get close to Mother, the stronger the force was that pushed me away.

Daddy came in behind her. My feelings must have shown. I could tell he wanted to cheer me up by the way he smiled.

"What's this?" He stuck his finger in my ear, pretending to look for something. "There's something in your ear, Ladybug."

I swatted his hand away.

"No, really, I'm serious," he said.

I laughed a little, even though it wasn't funny anymore. Daddy used to say "There's something in your ear" when I was little. I'd ask what it was, and he would say, "Oh, it's my finger!" Daddy needed to catch on that what was funny to me at age four wasn't so funny at twelve.

I walked into the kitchen to see Nanna. My stomach growled from the good smells.

My grandma had up and died the day Mother was born, and Grandpa had called Nanna, his younger sister, to come help with the baby. So Nanna never got married or had kids of her own. This all happened a long time ago, in Michigan, so I never met my grandpa before he died and hardly ever saw anyone else in Mother's family. Nanna'd just raised Mother, and now she was raising me.

"Hello, Lydia," Nanna said. Steam from the stove had caused a few long, white tendrils of hair to come loose from the braid she always coiled and pinned to the top of her head. Her round, flushed face looked happy to see me, but only for a second. Then she asked, "Did you finish your homework?"

"Yes, Nanna. My homework's all done." I gave her a kiss hello.

Her face smoothed back into a smile. "Well! That's fine. You'd best set the table. We don't want to be late for the . . ." Then she really looked at me. "Lydia Carson, what is that you're wearing?"

I looked down at my pants. Nanna hated pants on any girl. I'd have worn them tonight anyway, but I especially wanted to hide my bandaged knees.

"Nanna, you can't tell me the other girls will be wearing dresses to an outdoor movie!"

"I don't care what the other girls are wearing—" she began, but Mother walked into the kitchen and cut her off.

"Those dungarees are fine, Lydia. It might cool down and you'll be glad your legs are covered. Just change into a nicer blouse and you'll look as good as anyone in a dress."

"I don't know why I bother," Nanna said, pouring water into an ice-cube tray. "I tell you, one of these days I'm going to visit Louise and just not come back." Nanna visited her sister in Michigan for one week every summer and she threatened to move back there at least once a week.

"That's your choice," Mother said.

Nanna turned from setting the tray inside the freezer. She and Mother had a staring contest. Nanna was the first to look away. Sometimes I thought their bickering had more to do with what went on when Nanna was raising Mother than with me. I didn't care much, as long as whoever was on my side won.

I grabbed a stack of plates and silverware and headed into the dining room. I heard Mother say, "Glen tells me we have new neighbors. Have you met them?"

"Not yet," Nanna said. "They spent the afternoon unloading their belongings from their pickup truck. I thought I'd take a cake over tomorrow." Then her voice got louder so I'd hear, "Since tomorrow's Saturday, you can go with me, Lydia."

I almost dropped the plate I was holding. I started to argue, but with Nanna I'd learned that it was sometimes better to hold your tongue. She never forgot something if we argued about it.

The last thing I wanted was to be nose-to-nose with that Merrill boy and his ratty old raccoon. The more I thought about it, the more it seemed that his raccoon *did* look like an old rat, and seeing as how I didn't know the boy's name, "Ratboy" sounded as good as any. Besides, it made me smile and I figured he owed me a smile.

It took forever to get supper over with. It would never occur to Nanna to just make a quick meal of sandwiches. She had set out fried chicken, mashed potatoes, milk gravy, last summer's canned yellow beans cooked in bacon, bread-and-butter pickles, cornbread, and her homemade grape jelly.

"And we've got applesauce cake for dessert," she said as Daddy cleared the table.

Mother and Daddy groaned.

I couldn't take it. "Nanna, why can't we get a piece of pie or some ice cream downtown?"

"Because I could feed this family for a whole day on what dessert at the Oasis Café would cost."

Daddy spoke up. "Well, now, normally I'd agree with you, but Lydia does have a point. We really should spend some money downtown if we expect other folks to. Maybe we could have that delicious cake of yours tomorrow."

Nanna sniffed. "Fine. I'll just take it to the neighbors if no one in this family wants it. Save me work in the morning."

Shoot! There was no way Nanna would forget about visiting the neighbors with a whole applesauce cake staring at her.

We set out about half an hour before sunset. Daddy walked in front with a blanket draped over one arm and the other arm out for Nanna to hold. I walked behind with Mother. She had a camera strapped around her neck and was carrying a pad of paper with pencils stuck in her pockets to write an article about the Free Show. Mother acted as if interviewing people tonight would be work, but I knew better. Her mood always perked up when she had a story in the works for her paper. It could be something as small as a water main breaking and you'd find Mother there, happy as could be, taking pictures of the mess.

"This looks like a good spot. Girls, give me a hand," Daddy said, and tossed Mother and me each a corner of the blanket. We spread it out and he said, "Well, I'll leave you ladies now. I promised Sam I'd help him get the projector anchored in the window and such, since this is the first night."

I sat on our blanket and watched folks wander in and out of the stores, visiting and buying what-not before dark, when the movie would begin. Moms and dads were herding their youngsters like sheep through town. The kids ran from one store to another, pressing their noses into the windows. But once they caught sight of the library grounds, they made a beeline for it. Soon the grassy lot was speckled with blankets like ours.

Mother hadn't sat down since we got there. She was trying to get a few shots with her camera before dark. I don't know why she bothered. All she could photograph was either folks sitting on blankets or the Laundromat. I knew they were using the Laundromat wall as the movie screen, but I couldn't see how a blank wall would make an interesting picture. Then Mother went around interviewing people, asking what they thought about the Free Shows.

Nanna just sat on our blanket and complained. "Well,

they're going to have to put in some sort of seats here if they want me back, I can tell you that! How they expect people to sit on this old, hard ground long enough to watch a movie is beyond me!"

I looked about, thinking that anything would be better than sitting here listening to Nanna. I saw a group of little kids catching fireflies. I was too big for that. Then I saw a gathering of bigger kids.

"I'm going to see if Rae Anne is over there," I said to Nanna and ran off, pretending I couldn't hear her try to stop me.

I was disappointed when I didn't see Rae Anne, but there were a few kids my age.

"Hey, everybody! Whatcha doin'?" I asked.

"Soon as someone finds a can, we're playing kick-the-can."

When Junior Plunkett brought up a pork-and-beans can out of the neighbor's burn barrel, someone shouted to him, "You're it!" And we were off and running.

I hid behind the bushes in front of the library. I was almost the last person to be found. That worked in my favor, since Junior was getting tired of running back. We raced to the can and I kicked it a good one.

Suddenly I felt a sharp pain in the back of my shoulder. When I looked down, I saw a small rock roll to a stop.

I turned around, and there was chubby Bobby Wayans with a smug look on his face. Even though Bobby and I had pretty much been enemies for three years, I still couldn't see him doing something as bold as throwing a rock at me.

Then I saw that Ratboy step out of the shadows. He was tossing a small rock up and down in his hand. It was just like that yellow Bobby to befriend the new kid. But then, making a friend of someone who didn't know him was about the only chance Bobby had of getting one.

I knew that if Bobby had thrown the rock, I could have taken him in a fight. Heck, I'd have laid odds Nanna could take Bobby. I wasn't so sure I could take Ratboy, though, especially with my knees and backside sore from earlier today. Still, it never pays to show your fear.

"I hope you don't plan on signing up for Little League with that arm," I said. "I don't know what you were trying to hit, but I *know* you couldn't have meant to hit me with a rock."

"I hit what I aim at."

I looked around and made a face to the other kids as if to show how dumb that remark was. Then I put my hand on my chin and tapped it with my finger, pretending I was thinking real hard.

"Let's see. First he sends his pet rat over to climb up on me." I looked at the other kids. "I reckon that was to get acquainted with me, don't ya suppose? And when that doesn't work, he flings a pebble my way. Do y'all think this boy has a crush on me or what?"

Everybody started laughing, and Ratboy probably didn't cotton to being laughed at. His ears got red and his face followed suit.

He bellowed, "You've got to be the ugliest . . ." He sputtered, trying to find the right word. "*Girl* . . . I've ever laid eyes on. The only crush I've got on you is the one I'm going to give your skull if you don't pay up. You caused me to ruin my Popsicle today, and now I want my five cents for it."

That got my back up. "Your filthy animal ambushed me,

and you pushed me down. Now you expect money from me? I'll pay you when pigs fly!"

I pointed to Ratboy and said to the other kids, "If any of you see this pig hovering in the air, let me know. Then I'll think about giving him a nickel."

The other kids made a circle around him. Someone said, "So fly, already! Heck, *we'll* pay you a nickel to see that!"

With the crowd distracting Ratboy, I slowly began backing away. Suddenly hands clamped over my eyes from behind. Little prickles of fear crawled up my arms. Ratboy must have someone with him. I yanked the hands away and spun around.

"Rae Anne!" I yelled, and pure joy washed over me as I hugged my best friend.

"Didn't think I'd make it, did you?"

"I kept my fingers crossed that you would. You sure are a blessed sight." I noticed that she wore jeans, too, and hoped Nanna saw her.

"What're you playing?" she asked as she looked around me at Ratboy.

"We were playing kick-the-can, but it wasn't that much fun," I said. "Oh, look!"

Lights flickered on the Laundromat wall. When *Buck Rogers* came on, almost everyone clapped.

I held on to Rae Anne's hand and we watched the ten-minute serial. It ended right at the good part!

"Well, that sure was a short movie," she said.

"That's not the movie!" I told her. "Daddy said they're going to show ten minutes of *Buck Rogers* every week before the movie. That way, folks'll want to come back to see what happens next."

Rae Anne stuck out her bottom lip in a pout. "Well, that leaves me out. You know my mom and dad won't come every week."

"I'll memorize them and tell you every single thing that happens," I promised. "What do you want to do before the movie starts?"

She held out her hand. "Papa gave me money. How about we go get some ice cream?"

We ran over to the projector. Sam Green was on the inside and Daddy on the outside of the window. Daddy's face had that wrinkled-forehead look he gets when things don't go quite right.

"Daddy! Can I have some money for ice cream?" I was practically hopping, I was so happy Rae Anne was there.

He didn't say anything, just handed me a coin.

I could tell this wasn't the best time to bother him, but all he'd given me was a dime. "Add another one and I'll be able to crunch potato chips on top!"

Daddy let out a sigh. He reached into his pocket and gave me all his change—another dime, a nickel, and three pennies. "You're gonna have to ask Nanna or your mom for anything else. I'm busy here, Ladybug."

"Okay!" I gave Rae Anne a big smile, but I felt a little funny inside. He must really be having trouble with the movie because he almost always had time for me.

When Rae Anne put her arm through mine, though, I forgot all about Daddy and the movie. I looked up into the clear sky. The stars looked so bright and close I felt as if I could wave my arm and make them swirl around.

Smiling, I took a deep breath of the night air. I leaned into Rae Anne and said, "Isn't this the best night ever?"

As soon as the words were out of my mouth, I was yanked to a standstill. Someone had sneaked up and grabbed me by my hair. I always kept my hair pretty short, so it didn't hurt as much as it could have. It was the surprise of it that scared me more than anything.

Rae Anne let out a cry of shock. It wasn't until Ratboy whispered into my ear, "Hold still," that my fear and surprise turned to a blazing anger.

"Let go, you crazy hillbilly!"

I pawed at his hands. He let go of my hair and grabbed my arms, twisting them behind my back so tight that I went right to my knees. He was strong enough to hold both of my arms in one of his hands while he reached into my pocket.

What he wasn't counting on was Rae Anne. When I went down, he had to lower himself to one knee in order to fish around for my money. Rae Anne put her shoe on his rump and pushed him over.

She helped me scramble to my feet just in time to see Ratboy hold up a nickel and say, "I only take what's mine." Then he threw the rest of the money at me and ran away. Just like that—as if he hadn't hurt me and nearly scared me to death.

I was so mad I reached down and grabbed some of the coins, hurling them after him. I wanted to scream but I couldn't. To my horror, great racking sobs came from me. I hate to cry. I'd do anything before I'd let someone see me cry, even someone I trust as much as Rae Anne. I sat down on the curb and rubbed my sore head until the tears stopped.

Rae Anne picked up the money. She was fired up from the fight, asking a blue million questions. "What was that all about? Who is he? Why would he do that just for a nickel?"

And when I didn't answer right away, she said, "We have to tell your dad!"

I cleared the lump out of my throat. "No. I don't want to tell anyone and I want you to swear that you won't, either."

"Lydia! You were attacked! We *have* to tell."

"He moved into your grandma's house. I'm going to have to see him every day."

"Oh, Lydia, *that's* who rented Grandma's house?"

"Yeah." I wiped my eyes on my sleeve. "I don't want him thinking I run to my daddy every time something goes wrong. He'll call me a baby and never leave me alone. I'll handle this my own way."

I had lost all taste for ice cream and the Free Show. This boy was meaner than a snake and had the strength to back it up. Just thinking about living next door to a bully made my throat feel tight and my eyes sting. I hated that feeling. It meant I was close to crying again.

We walked back to the library lot. Rae Anne slid down on the blanket where Mother and Nanna were sitting. I knew she wanted me to say something, but she was a good enough friend to keep quiet about it. Daddy was standing next to the blanket. He looked so tall and strong. I slid my hand into his and, without looking, he gave it a squeeze. I was glad he was staring at the movie. I got so much comfort from just being at his side and touching him that I didn't want him to ruin it by asking what was wrong.

Finally he said, "Well, we're going to have to call an emergency city council meeting to get more money. This setup just won't do it. We've got to find a way to mount that projector straight. Nobody's going to watch a show this way, even if it *is* free."

I looked out over a sea of Maywood folks with their heads all tilted to the left as Gene Autry rode his horse, Champion, through the cracks of the Laundromat wall straight toward the sky.

"I'm tired." I yawned as we walked into the kitchen after the show was over.

"Too much fun for one night, Ladybug?" Daddy asked as he knelt down to kiss my cheek. He was in a talkative mood now. People had enjoyed themselves and the merchants of Maywood had made money, even if the movie hadn't turned out straight. It would be a while before everyone went to bed. I just wanted to be alone.

"I guess so, Daddy. Good night."

"Good night," Mother mumbled as she pulled out a kitchen chair, not even looking at me.

I walked toward the stairs, when Nanna pulled me to her. I could smell the lilac perfume she usually saved for church as she squeezed me into her softness.

"Good night, baby."

It didn't matter how stern or strict Nanna was with me during the day, at bedtime she poured all the love she had into her good-nights.

From my bedroom I could hear Daddy, Nanna, and Mother in the kitchen reliving the evening. To hear Nanna talk about the good time she had, you would have thought the whole thing was her idea. After all that complaining I'd had to listen to! I heard Mother once say that Nanna worked like a hot water faucet. You had to let the water run a long time before it got warm, but then it went straight to hot.

As I listened to them, I wondered what I was going to do

about Ratboy. It had always been my way to handle things on my own. Daddy's turn-the-other-cheek attitude didn't sit well with me, and Nanna would just try to turn Ratboy and me into friends. The thought of that made my skin crawl. The truth is, I was a little bit afraid of Ratboy. Fear was something I couldn't allow, so I did what I always did when I needed to gather up my courage: I lay there in bed and talked to Robert.

Robert was Mother's son and he was dead, but I didn't let a thing like that stop me.

3

I had learned about Robert accidentally. It wasn't something I was brought up knowing. Two years before—the spring I was ten years old—I had overheard Daddy and Nanna talking. I had walked into the house as noisy as ever, but they'd been deep in their conversation and hadn't heard me.

"Glen, we go through this every spring and you know it. Evelyn mopes around like she's the only person in this house. Lost in her own world, she is." Nanna made quick swipes back and forth across the floor with her broom the way she always did when she was agitated.

"I know, but she doesn't want to talk about it. We need to have patience."

"How much patience, Glen? He's been dead for over thirteen years. It's time that girl realizes she has a family here and now."

"Who died?" I asked.

Nanna looked up and her hand flew to her chest. For once she didn't have a single thing to say.

"Who died, Daddy?"

He coughed, stalling for time. "You know, Ladybug, I was just thinking the mushrooms ought to be up. How about we head over to Trotter's woods and see what we can find?" Which meant he'd tell me, but he'd take his own sweet time about it.

We walked through the woods with him naming different bugs and plants, and in the same soft tone of voice he used to tell me the difference between poison ivy and poison oak, he said, "Your mother was married when she was young. She had a boy named Robert, and about thirteen years ago, he died."

"She did? I didn't know that."

"Well, there's more. Her husband died, too. Her first husband."

Another husband? I always knew Mother was older than Daddy, but I never knew she had had a whole other *family* before she had us! "What happened?"

"It was springtime and Robert was eager to go out on a lake fishing with his friend. Your mother said no. He wasn't a strong swimmer."

Daddy found a log and sat down. "When he didn't show up for supper, your mother got worried and called his friend's house. She found out they had gone fishing anyway, so her husband drove out to the lake.

"Robert's friend later said that he and Robert had been

goofing off, standing in the boat and all. When it overturned, Robert panicked. His friend tried to help him but couldn't get him to the boat. Robert went under, and that's when his father saw them. He tried to swim to them but never made it to the boat. Turned out he had a heart attack trying to save his boy."

"Holy cow!" I let that sink in for a minute. "How old was Robert?"

"Fourteen years old. Still a baby."

I bridled at that.

"I didn't know your mother then, of course. When she came here to Maywood that was all behind her. But every spring reminds her of her loss and she gets the blues."

Daddy looked hard at me and said, "Your mother was so grief-stricken after losing both her husband and Robert the same day that she doesn't even remember their funerals. All this has been more than she could deal with."

I tried to imagine how awful it would feel to be so upset that you wouldn't even remember a funeral.

Daddy went on. "She moved to Maywood to get a new start. That's when I met her." He stood and picked up the sack of mushrooms. "I don't want anyone tearing the scabs off those wounds of hers. Promise me you won't talk about this to your mother."

"I promise," I said. But I didn't promise I wouldn't ask Nanna.

When he dropped me off at the house, I ran in and threw the sack of mushrooms on the counter. "Nanna, tell me about Robert."

She must have been wanting to talk about him for a long time because she didn't shush me at all.

"That scamp." She lowered herself into a kitchen chair, shaking her head as she sat there remembering. "Robert was handsome as the devil and every bit as mischievous. He was always up to something, like the time he climbed the water tower."

"Water tower!"

"When your mother got married, she moved from Michigan to Ohio. She didn't work then, so she didn't need me. I was staying with my sister, Louise, but your mother wrote to me often, so I knew a lot about Robert's escapades. This one happened when he was a couple years older than you. It seems the boys in town would climb the water tower and paint their names on the side of it. Robert was too young for that, and it's a dangerous thing to do at any age. But he decided he would do it someday anyway, so he might as well do it when he was twelve. That would make him the youngest boy ever to climb the water tower."

Robert was taking on heroic proportions in my mind.

"Once he was spotted, a crowd gathered to watch. Your mother heard all the commotion, came outside, and saw a boy climbing the tower. When she found out it was Robert, she nearly fainted. She stood waiting, barely daring to breathe until Robert's feet were planted back on Ohio soil. She was mad at him and said she cried something awful, probably from fear and relief that he was safe."

I thought about that. It was one thing for Nanna to be smitten with Robert. Nanna loved lots of people. It was another to imagine Mother so worried about him that she would cry "something awful." I didn't know of one tear she'd ever shed over me. I wondered why Mother cared so much about Robert. Was it because he was a boy?

Nanna leaned close and said, "You'll never believe what he did next."

She didn't notice what her words were doing to me. She was too wrapped up in her story.

"Lydia?" Nanna asked. "Are you listening to me?"

"Oh, yes, ma'am."

"Robert was sent to his room, but he climbed out his bedroom window and sneaked the clothes basket off the back porch. He went around the neighborhood filling that basket with every yellow flower he could find: daylilies, daffodils, even dandelions. He knew how much your mother loved flowers, especially yellow ones."

It made me feel funny that Robert had known Mother loved yellow flowers and I hadn't.

"Then he set the basket of flowers on the front porch with a note stuck on top that said, 'I wanted to do it, so I did it. I just never meant to make you cry.' "

Nanna took off her glasses and dabbed her eyes with the corner of her apron. She said, "Now, how could you stay mad at a kid like that?"

Nanna had raised me since I was a baby. I knew she loved me, but if you looked up the word "strict" in the dictionary, you'd see Nanna's picture. If I got into trouble, then sneaked out after she'd sent me to my room, she'd probably put bars on my window. Yet Robert could do what he did, leave a note that didn't even say he was sorry, and Nanna couldn't stay mad at him. I felt glad he wasn't around anymore.

Nanna wiped her floury hands on her apron and walked over to the cabinet that held her cookie tins. She took down one of the tins, pulled out a picture, folded it in half, and ripped it in two.

"Nanna! What are you doing?"

She handed me half of the picture and said, "I'm showing you your brother."

My brother! The bitterness I was feeling toward Robert eased when she used the word "brother." I hadn't thought of him as that. Just a part of Mother's life a long time ago.

The picture showed a smiling boy squatting on one knee and holding a trophy of some sort. He had the same dark, wavy hair I do, but the thing that set me back on my heels was Robert's eyes. In the picture they looked almost white, as if there wasn't any color at all. My eyes are a light blue, but some people call them gray. I was thinking how Robert looked so much like me, we could be brother and sister. I laughed out loud when I realized how funny that was.

I'd almost hated Robert a few minutes before, but thinking of him as my brother changed things somehow. I hugged the picture to me as if I'd been given a new toy. But I was still puzzled by what Nanna had done. "Why did you tear the picture in half?"

"It's the only one I have, and it was taken with his daddy. We don't have any business discussing *him*."

I didn't see what that had to do with anything, but I didn't really pay it any mind at the time. I kept my promise to Daddy and never mentioned Robert's name to Mother. And I put my picture of him in an envelope taped under my sock drawer so she wouldn't accidentally stumble across it.

I'd thought a lot about Robert in the two years since that day. At first I couldn't wait to tell Rae Anne. She had a big brother, Darryl. She used to fight with him when they were younger, but that all changed when Darryl went into the army.

Darryl never got cross with Rae Anne anymore, and he looked tall and handsome in his uniform—a regular Elvis Presley, straight out of the movie *G.I. Blues*. When he came home on leave, he'd put the top down on his convertible and take us girls for rides in his car as he cruised around visiting old friends. Rae Anne and I would pretend we were Audrey Hepburn and put scarves around our hair, wear sunglasses, and crank the radio up as loud as it would go.

I had always wanted a big brother just like Rae Anne's. Here Nanna had just handed me one. Yet I couldn't get the words out when I tried to tell Rae Anne about Robert. Keeping him to myself made him seem as if he were just mine somehow.

Whenever something happened that made me feel I could use a little courage, like my run-in with Ratboy, for instance, I sneaked my picture of Robert out of its hiding place and talked to him. Knowing about Robert made me braver somehow. It made me feel that, even if I couldn't exactly touch him, I wasn't alone.

"Lydia! Your breakfast is getting cold."

I opened my eyes when I heard Nanna's voice. I rolled over to look at the clock and the back of my head throbbed. The pain brought back the memory of Ratboy pulling my hair last night. I rubbed my head and tried to look at the clock again. There was Robert's picture on my nightstand. I had drifted off to sleep before I put it back. I grabbed the picture and jumped up. For two years, I had kept my promise to Daddy not to mention Robert to Mother, and I didn't aim to break that promise now.

I hurried over and pulled open my sock drawer. Before tucking the picture back in the envelope underneath, I took one more look at my brother. I rubbed my finger over his face and said, "If the same blood that runs in your veins runs in mine, how can I let a little thing like a no-account bully scare me?"

That thought got me dressed and ready to meet Ratboy face-to-face.

4

"I'm sure our new neighbors are busy enough without having to entertain on their second day here." Mother was still in her bathrobe.

"It's a friendly gesture, Evelyn. It's just what you do when you have new neighbors," Nanna said.

"Well, I plan to spend the morning writing an article about the Free Show while it's still fresh in my mind." Mother sat down with her legal pad and pencil. Nanna's orders didn't carry the same weight with Mother that they did me.

Nanna just said, "Suit yourself," and let it go. I wished she'd say "Suit yourself" to me just once in my life, especially today. Instead, by nine o'clock she had me standing on the Merrills' front porch, with a scrubbed face and holding the applesauce cake.

"Yes?" Mrs. Merrill answered the knock.

Nanna said, "How do! I'm Lydia Baldwin and I live next door, but please call me Nanna—everyone does."

"Oh . . . hello!"

"What's all that racket?" a deep voice bellowed from inside the house.

Mrs. Merrill's face turned beet red and instead of inviting us in, she slid out onto the porch and quickly closed the screen door behind her. I didn't know where those people were from, but not inviting a person into your home was a downright insult in Maywood. Nanna pretended not to notice and kept on talking.

"This is my niece, Lydia Carson—my namesake." Nanna threw that in whenever she could. "And we just wanted to welcome you to our little town by bringing this cake over."

"Oh, gracious! Thank you so much!" For someone who hadn't seemed all that friendly, Mrs. Merrill sure was tickled by that cake.

"Boys! Beth! Come here, please."

The moment I'd been dreading came when Ratboy showed up with a taller boy and a little girl.

Mrs. Merrill said, "I'm Carolyn Merrill." She put her hands on the little girl's shoulders and said, "And this is Elizabeth. We call her Beth." She pointed to the boys and said, "This is Elliot and his brother, Willis."

So Ratboy's name was Willis. I kept my eyes on Elliot, the older boy, but I was tuned into Ratboy more than if I'd looked straight at him.

"Hi, Elliot," I said.

His mouth turned up on one side in a half smile and he said, "Hi."

Then I turned to Willis. He just looked right back at me. No way was I going to be friendly to that maniac.

Nanna nudged me forward. "Aren't you going to say hello?"

If I acted nasty or said what was really on my mind, Nanna would drag me home by my ear. I finally just nodded. A nod would be easy to take back if need be, but a "Hello" was something altogether different. Ratboy nodded back.

"Elliot, would you bring out the kitchen chairs," Mrs. Merrill said in a low voice. Then she stood there beaming at us, as if not inviting people into your home was the most normal thing in the world. The oldest boy, Elliot, quietly took the cake inside and brought out two kitchen chairs.

The porch ran across the whole front of the house. Elliot set the chairs at one end, under the hooks where Rae Anne's grandparents, Mr. and Mrs. Ogle, used to hang their porch swing in the summer. Seeing those hooks made me long for Mrs. Ogle and Rae Anne.

"Carolyn, I need to go now," Elliot said. Then he turned to Nanna. "Nice meetin' ya, ma'am."

He nodded at me and ran down the steps. I hoped Willis would excuse himself next. No such luck. He sat like a lump on the other end of the porch, so I moved to the steps and sat there. The little girl, Beth, ran over and sat close to me. I figured she wanted to get as far away from Willis as she could, too.

Mrs. Merrill whispered, "Please have a seat, Mrs. Baldwin. Could I offer you a glass of water?"

Nanna matched Mrs. Merrill's low voice. "Oh, thank you, no. We just finished breakfast. Please call me Nanna—everyone does. And it's *Miss* Baldwin, actually. I never did get around to marrying. I was too busy, I guess. I raised my brother's daughter, Lydia's mother, after his wife died. And I'm helping to raise Lydia since her mother and daddy both work."

"Oh! You sound like me! Except that I did get married, but Willis and Elliot aren't mine. They're my husband's boys. We got married a few months ago . . ." Mrs. Merrill just let the sentence drift off. She looked scared, as if she'd said too much when she hadn't really said anything at all.

Nanna reached out and put a hand on Mrs. Merrill's arm. "So you're raising your husband's boys. How nice they have you. And is Beth your stepchild, too?"

"Oh, no!" Mrs. Merrill looked so relieved that it was almost painful to look at her. "Beth is my daughter from my first marriage."

"Well, she sure is a pretty thing," Nanna said. "Just like her mother. You have the most beautiful hair."

Mrs. Merrill's cheeks turned bright pink.

"I don't recall hearing of any Merrills from around Maywood," Nanna said. "Did you travel far?"

"We lived in Kentucky before coming here. Boyd heard of a factory job in Aylesville, so here we are."

Nanna smiled and nodded. Then she said, "My lands! I just remembered that I left the milk at home. Why, you can't give someone an applesauce cake without milk to wash it down. Lydia, would you please go get the milk in the refrigerator that I bought for the Merrills?"

Milk! Whoever heard of taking milk to someone's house? But Nanna was giving me that look that told me it was an order, so I just said, "Yes, ma'am. Be right back."

I flew down the steps and back to our house, happy to get away from Ratboy's porch, even if just for a few minutes.

There was only one carton of milk in our refrigerator, and it was already open. I didn't know why Nanna lied about buying milk for the neighbors, but she'd never lie unless she had a good reason. I dug around the cupboards until I found a pitcher that was big enough to hold the milk. That way Mrs. Merrill wouldn't know Nanna hadn't bought it especially for them.

I walked slowly so as not to splash the milk, and that meant I could hear Nanna talking, too.

"And we go to the United Methodist church every Sunday. I was raised a Baptist, but my nephew is a Methodist to the bone, so I go along. You're welcome to come. It's a nice walk in the summertime, just four blocks to the east and one block south. If you like, you can come with us once you get settled in."

I looked up at Mrs. Merrill. She had the most excited look on her face listening to Nanna. It was a pretty face with big brown eyes, and Nanna was right about her hair—it turned under just like Jackie Kennedy's. She could have passed for Willis and Elliot's big sister. Pretty as she was, though, there was something about her face that bothered me—something I couldn't quite put my finger on. Then it hit me. Some people don't show their feelings on their face, but Mrs. Merrill's face showed too much.

I handed Nanna the pitcher.

"Thank you, Lydia." Nanna looked me straight in the eye as if to say she really meant it. "And here you go, Carolyn."

Nanna handed Mrs. Merrill the pitcher of milk, then said, "Well, I need to get on home now. Housework never waits, but you know all about that, don't you, dear? Now, don't forget—I'm right next door if you need an egg or directions or even some company. I'm always there, you hear?"

I wondered why on earth Mrs. Merrill's eyes would shine with tears over someone offering her an egg or directions.

At the thought of leaving, my breath started coming at a normal pace for the first time since the visit had started. I hopped off the porch, ready to bolt for home, when Nanna said, "Lydia, you come home in an hour. We don't want to wear out our welcome, but I know you and Willis will want to get acquainted."

"Nanna!" I said, much too loud. "I'd better help with the housework. Willis and I met yesterday, so we've already talked." I looked at him out of the corner of my eye, and he looked at me as if nothing bad had passed between us.

"Oh, honey, I know how you've longed for someone to play with. I wouldn't dream of tearing you away from your new friend. Carolyn, send her on home in an hour or so."

I watched helplessly as Nanna walked away, abandoning me at the devil's door. I couldn't tear my eyes off her back until I felt Beth tugging at my arm.

"Want to see my doll?"

I want to go home! my mind screamed. But Beth shoved her doll into my hand. It was buck-naked, with most of its hair gone. What was left had a kind of hard feel and was sticking straight up.

"Where are her clothes?" I asked.

Beth stood there sucking on her pointer finger the way some kids suck their thumbs.

"Don't you have doll clothes for her?" I tried again.

Instead of answering, Beth said, "Look what she can do!" She grabbed the doll and tilted her. One of her eyes closed, but the other was stuck open. It sure was a sorry excuse for a doll. Still, Beth seemed so proud of her that I found myself saying, "Well, what do you know. She can wink!"

Beth laughed, then asked, "Want to see Zorro?"

She grabbed my hand and pulled me around to the back-yard. Willis hopped down and ran ahead of us.

"Who's Zorro?" I asked as she pulled me over to where Willis stood beside a rusty rabbit hutch. Inside the hutch was his old raccoon.

"That's Zorro!" Beth said, giggling and clapping her hands.

I had to admit that Zorro was a good name, what with the dark fur around the animal's eyes making him look like Zorro, the masked avenger from TV. "Oh, I've already seen Zorro." I tried to look bored.

"Don't touch him," Willis said.

"Don't worry. I *never* wanted to touch that dumb old rat of yours."

"He ain't a rat. I'd wager he's smarter than you." Willis pushed by me and opened the door. The coon ran out of its cage. Willis looked me right in the eye with a smirk on his face. I matched him stare for stare. Willis gave a real nasty smile and slowly lowered himself to the ground. Then I knew I'd been had. That old raccoon ran right up his back!

My blood boiled when I remembered yesterday. "I thought you said he didn't run up backs." I tried to keep my voice steady.

"I never said that," Willis drawled. "What I said was, he wouldn't run up *your* scrawny back."

My face flamed hot with anger and I shouted, "That whole mess was your fault. I didn't do one thing wrong yesterday. If you'd kept your filthy pet in his cage, none of that would have happened."

Willis stuck his face right into mine and yelled, "He's cleaner than you, and you'd better get used to him. I don't think I'll put him in his cage a'tall now, 'cept maybe to sleep."

Willis was just a few inches from me, but I didn't flinch when I shouted back, "You know, you might be right about him being clean. I thought that stench I smelled was coming from him, but now that we're nose-to-nose I see who really stinks around here."

I couldn't stand to look at his ugly, freckly face for a minute more. I headed for the fence that separated our yards. When I thought of the money Willis had taken last night, I got even madder. I yelled over my shoulder, "And I don't know where you're from, but around here if you drop your Popsicle, it's your own fault. Nobody owes you money for it."

"Popsicle! You got to buy a Popsicle, Willis?" Beth asked.

"No. She's half crazy."

"Hah! You think I'm crazy?" I didn't get to say anything else because Beth started yelling at Willis.

"You bought a Popsicle and you were s'posed to bring *all* the money home. That pop-bottle money was for groceries, Willis! I'm telling!"

Before Willis could grab her, she ran in the back screen door. Willis put his hands on top of his head and spun around as if looking for a way to escape.

Then the back door blew open with a bang and a man I figured must be his daddy charged out the door.

"Boyd, no! Please!" Mrs. Merrill cried as she ran after her husband. When she saw me, she flapped her hands in the air as if to shoo me away. "Lydia! It's time to go on home now!"

I climbed up the fence, jumped into our yard, and watched Mr. Merrill pull his belt from his pants. He made it into a loop and held it in one hand as he chased Willis. Mr. Merrill looked mad as all get-out. Willis made a break for it and ran down the street.

I headed for our house. I really thought Willis needed a taste of his own medicine, but I couldn't help feeling a chill thinking that Mr. Merrill might actually use that belt on Willis. I'd never seen anybody get whipped. Surely Mr. Merrill was just trying to scare him.

I heard Nanna talking to Mother before I got to the back door. "I could be wrong, but it's my guess that the milk and cake we just took over is all the food that's in that house right now. And if I'm not mistaken, I'd say those kitchen chairs are the only things they have to sit on. Oh, Evelyn, it was sad."

"How do you know they only have kitchen chairs? Maybe their furniture hasn't arrived yet. Maybe she hasn't been to the grocery store. Really, Nanna!" I could see Mother through the screen door, crossing out what she'd written with an angry slash of her pencil.

"Well, if you had bothered to go, you'd know what I was talking about."

I scuffed my feet real loud on the back porch so they'd know I was there. Nanna saw me and reached for the coffee tin that held the grocery money. She counted out some change. "Lydia, I'm going to need you to run to Hanson's A&P to get some milk. Make sure they put it in a sack for you. That Fred Hanson is so tight with his money he won't put just one item in a sack unless you ask."

I figured she wanted the milk in a sack so Mrs. Merrill wouldn't see me bringing it home and catch her in the lie about buying milk for them.

"Here's some extra money for an ice cream Drumstick. I know how much you like them."

Nanna never gave me money for something like ice cream. I knew she was repaying me for not acting funny about giving the Merrills our milk. Normally I would have snatched that money up and run all the way for an ice cream Drumstick.

"No thanks, Nanna. I'll just get the milk. And I'll make sure they put it in a sack."

I didn't like Willis any more today than I had yesterday, but thinking about him getting into trouble for something as little as spending a nickel on a Popsicle made my insides feel funny.

5

As soon as I finished my pancakes and bacon, I ran upstairs to get ready for church. Nanna never let me put on my church clothes until after I finished breakfast because she said I always wore whatever I ate. I wanted to remind her that I wasn't a little kid now and knew how to use a napkin. But I figured the first time I ate in my church clothes, I'd spill a whole glass of milk down my front.

I jerked a prissy dress with a starched collar over my head and clomped downstairs in my good shoes.

Mother was in the kitchen tying Daddy's necktie for him. Usually she still had her robe on when we left, but this morning she'd dressed in her gardening clothes.

"It's a nice morning for planting," Daddy said.

"I know! It's been such a lovely week. I've been itching to get my petunias in the ground."

"It'd be nice if you were itching to sing praises to the Lord," Nanna mumbled.

Mother rolled her eyes and Daddy gave her shoulder a squeeze. We went through this every Sunday morning. Mother never went with us, Nanna always grumbled about it, and Daddy tried to keep the peace.

The only times I know of that Mother stepped foot in

church was when she married Daddy and when she went to the mother-daughter banquet held every year on the last Sunday in May. For that, she never put up a fuss, because it meant so much to Nanna to have her there. Whether Mother liked it or not, Nanna was the only mama she had ever known.

Nanna salted a roast and slid it into the oven so it would be ready when we came back. The one good thing about Sunday was eating that big meal at noon instead of having to wait until the end of the day.

"Get your Bible, young lady," Nanna said. "And hurry! We don't want to be late."

I clomped back upstairs and grabbed my Bible. I hurried out my bedroom door, running right into Mother.

"Oh! I'm sorry!"

"I wasn't watching where I was going," she said. "I'm so anxious to get outdoors that I left my new gardening gloves in my room."

We stood there for an awkward minute, until she turned to go into her bedroom. Staying home on Sunday morning and working in the garden sounded more like heaven than anything Pastor Owen was going to say about it. But I knew better than to ask Mother if I could stay home. Even if she said yes—which she wouldn't—Nanna and Daddy would have fits. They never missed church for anything.

When Mother came back out of her room, tearing the tags off her new gloves, her face looked flushed, as if she really was happy to get to work on those flowerbeds. It made me think I might be able to ask her a question that had been weighing on my mind. "Mother?"

"Yes?"

"Well, I don't really like church, either. But"—I squeezed the Bible hard and croaked out—"I've been wondering . . . Why don't you ever go with us?"

I made myself stand very still. I didn't want to fidget.

She took a deep breath and looked around the hall, as if she might find the answer there. Finally she said, "God and I parted ways a long time ago, Lydia."

I slowly walked downstairs thinking about that. I didn't much care for the fuss of church, but God was a whole other story.

Monday morning came before I was ready for it, but then Monday morning has a way of doing that when it's a school day.

As soon as the class finished saying the Pledge, Mrs. Warren was called into the hall. My head held up my desk lid while I searched for my science book. She came back into the room and said, "Class, I'd like you to meet our new student, Willis Merrill."

I rose out of that desk so fast the bang of the lid could have been heard all the way to Chicago. Sure enough, there stood Willis with Mrs. Warren on one side of him and his brother, Elliot, on the other. At least I knew his daddy hadn't killed him for spending that nickel.

Mrs. Warren fiddled with her brooch the way she always did when she was happy, mad, or just plain thinking. "Willis, we'll need to have a desk moved in for you. All our desks are full right now, but you may take a chair from the reading area and sit . . ."

Bobby Wayans sat third seat back, same as me, but on the

other side of the room. I heard his whiny voice saying, "Mrs. Warren? Oh, Mrs. Warren? Willis can sit with me. I'll be happy to share my books and desk with him."

"Oh, Bobby, what a nice gesture. Yes, Willis, why don't you sit with Bobby? He's one of our best students. I'm sure you'll get along beautifully."

You could have hung coats on the sides of Bobby's mouth, they were turned up so high into a smile. Nobody could stand Bobby's mealymouthed ways for long, and it had been years since anybody'd tried. Bobby was almost giddy as he ushered Willis to his desk.

When I looked back at the door, Elliot was walking out. Maywood Junior-Senior High School was one block away on the other side of the ball diamond, and he was probably headed there to enroll himself. I wondered why Elliot had come instead of Willis's daddy or his stepmother. But more than that, I wondered why on earth anybody would start school just two weeks before summer vacation.

All in all, the morning went pretty smoothly, considering the kids kept craning their necks to get a look at Willis. Mrs. Warren didn't call on him, so he just sat quietly at Bobby's desk. It was lunch that I was dreading.

Rae Anne was on me the second the bell rang. "He's in our class!"

"Gee whiz, Rae Anne. What was your first clue?"

"Well, you didn't tell me he'd be in our class! Poor you. There's just no escaping with him being your neighbor, too."

"Is reminding me of that supposed to make me feel better?"

"Sorry. Who was that with him?"

"You've gone to school with Bobby Wayans your whole life and you forgot his name?"

"Not him, silly. I mean that cute guy. Was that his brother?"

"Well, yeah, that's Elliot. What's got into you, calling him cute?"

"He's sure better-looking than Willis, you've got to give him that!" she said.

Picking up my lunch tray, I said, "Willis's raccoon is better looking than he is."

We sat down, and Bobby sat at the table next to us with Willis. Bobby looked proud as a peacock sitting among boys who wouldn't normally give him the time of day.

I took a bite of my lunch and heard Bobby say, "Go on, Willis. Tell the guys how you taught your raccoon to do tricks. Tell them about how he'll ride piggy-back style."

"You've got a pet coon?" one of the boys asked.

Willis just nodded.

Another said, "Bring him to the next Free Show. Would he ride on my back?"

I snorted loud enough for them to hear me.

Willis whispered something to Bobby, then Bobby said, "Willis says he's particular about whose back he'll touch. For instance, Willis said his raccoon wouldn't ride Lydia Carson's back if she tied bait around her neck!"

Everyone at the table laughed. Doing a slow burn, I picked up my napkin and put a blob of green Jell-O in it. "Watch this," I said to Rae Anne. I walked right over to Bobby and Willis, picked up my napkin, and said, "Ah-ah-ah-choo!" blowing into the napkin on the "choo" part. Green Jell-O sprayed all over the back of Bobby's head. The whole cafeteria roared with laughter.

It was a pity Jell-O hadn't landed on Willis, too. I'd have to think up something else for him.

After lunch we all filed back in for our history lesson.

"Class, get out your history books, please, and turn to chapter 34." Mrs. Warren was still smiling "the smile." She'd been wearing it since Willis and Elliot had shown up this morning. It was a smile I'd seen before. She wore it on Parents' Night or when the principal observed our class. I didn't know a new student would rate the smile, but then we'd never had a new student before.

"Willis, we are reading about the industrial revolution. If Bobby would be kind enough to let you borrow his book, I'd like you to read the first page, please."

Willis just sat there. Bobby hurried to find the page and handed him the book. Willis gave Bobby a lazy look, then crossed his arms instead of taking it.

You could see the first crack in the smile. Mrs. Warren fingered her brooch and said, "Um, Willis, here at Maywood Grade School we stand up to read. I know different schools have different ways, but that's our way. You may stand now and read the first page of chapter thirty-four."

Willis looked down at the fingernails on one of his hands as if checking to see whether it was nail-clipping time. The rest of us turned our heads from Willis to Mrs. Warren. Her face was as red as the lipstick she wore.

"Willis, do you have a hearing problem that I wasn't made aware of?" She seemed to genuinely hope he did.

"No. I hear just fine."

"Then stand and read."

Nothing.

"Now!"

Willis crossed his arms and kept his eyes on the desk in front of him. The longer he sat and stared, the more irate Mrs. Warren looked. All three of her chins quivered as she marched her considerable self to the side of Bobby's desk. For once I felt a little sorry for Bobby. He'd never been in the vicinity of trouble before. Even though it was Willis our teacher was after, I'll bet Bobby darn near peed his pants.

Mrs. Warren put both hands on the desk and her face right in Willis's. She used her quiet voice, which was ever so much scarier than her loud voice.

"Willis Merrill, I do not tolerate this kind of behavior in my classroom. When I ask a student to do something, that student had better do it or have a very good reason not to. You're new today. In light of that, I'm giving you one more chance than I would anyone else. Is there a reason you refuse to read?"

It was deadly quiet. I could hear the blood pounding in my ear. A quick look around the room told me that everyone's eyes were locked on Willis. We all knew that when Mrs. Warren talked like that, the only thing that would save you was vomiting, right then and there. Anything short of that, you were a walking dead kid.

Despite my feelings for Willis, I wished he'd just read and get it over with.

"Willis," Mrs. Warren tried again, "your choices are to read or visit the principal."

Willis slumped a little and raised his head. I was surprised to see him look so weary, like a person who'd been in too many battles. Then, almost as fast as it came, the expression left and he slowly sat back. First he looked at Bobby, then he looked around the room, and finally his eyes fell on Mrs. Warren.

"What would you have done for fun today if it wasn't for me comin' to this school? Pulled wings off flies? Picked on Tubby here?" He pointed to Bobby. "Seems to me you oughta have better things to do than yank my chain."

"Huhhh!" Mrs. Warren's intake of breath could be heard above all twenty-five of ours.

"And how about you take a step back, 'cause that per-fume of yours is makin' my eyes water."

Mrs. Warren's hand shot out quicker than a serpent's tongue. She grabbed Willis's ear, twisted it, and pulled up. Willis had to either stand or knock her hand off his ear. I'd have bet the farm he would have fought her, but not being as dumb as I thought, he chose to stand. She didn't let go either. "Now march!" she said, leading him out of the room.

When Mrs. Warren came back, she didn't say one word about Willis. It drove everybody crazy wondering what happened to him. As far as I was concerned, no punishment was too severe. Willis was just plain ornery, and this time the whole sixth-grade class and Mrs. Warren had been there to see it.

I'd been able to get my homework done at school while Mrs. Warren had Willis in the principal's office, so I got home earlier than usual—just in time to see Willis and his coon take off. I ran upstairs and changed out of my school dress into some real clothes. Running back down, I swung wide over the newel post and jumped—but landed no closer than ever to the linen closet door. Since Nanna wasn't in the kitchen, I grabbed a couple of buttermilk cookies and looked out the back door.

Nanna was leaning over the fence holding a sack out to Mrs. Merrill. You'd have thought the sack had live snakes in it the way Mrs. Merrill held back, seemingly scared of touching it.

I gently opened the door and crouched low beside the steps, listening to Nanna and Mrs. Merrill as I nibbled on a cookie.

"Carolyn, it's a shame to throw these seed potatoes and onion sets away. Please take them. We've got all we need in our garden."

"I just don't know . . ." Mrs. Merrill said in that vague way she had.

"Look over there." Nanna pointed to where Mr. and Mrs. Ogle had had their garden. "The Ogles grew some of the biggest vegetables in town in that patch of ground. It may seem like work now, but it will be worth it once the garden starts producing."

"It's not the work. It's . . . I need to ask Boyd if it's okay," Mrs. Merrill said, looking down at her feet.

"I'll take that sack, ma'am." We all turned when we heard Elliot's voice. He cleared his throat and said, "Carolyn's probably unsure about it because we don't have any hoes or rakes."

"Well, land sakes," Nanna said, "you can borrow ours if that's all that's keeping you from a garden!"

"Ma'am, I would appreciate you lending me your garden tools, but I can't do it unless you let me pay you back," Elliot said. "How about if I weed your garden for the summer? Would that be a fair deal to you?"

"Oh, honey, Mr. Carson takes care of the garden," Nanna answered. "It's really not necessary."

"Then I can't accept your offer, ma'am."

I looked from Elliot back to Nanna. He was messing with Nanna's job chart. She had some peculiar ideas about how our household should be run. Nanna did everything around our house and wouldn't accept help from Mother or Daddy. She did, however, expect Mother to keep up the flower beds and Daddy to mow the lawn and do the vegetable garden. Come summer, I was to hang the clothes on the line. Heaven forbid if Mother made her own bed or pulled a weed as she walked by the garden.

I figured it must really be important to Nanna that the Merrills have a garden when she said, "All right, Elliot, you have yourself a deal. I'm sure Mr. Carson could use your help in the garden. The shed is unlocked and you just help yourself to the tools. You'll need to get busy, though. This is planting season."

"Thank you, ma'am. Thank you very much!" Elliot took the sack of dirty old seed potatoes from Nanna as if it were a really nice gift.

"Well, then, I'll go on in and finish cooking supper." Nanna sounded plumb worn out from the work of talking them into a garden.

I scooted around the corner of the house until Nanna was inside. There wasn't any sign of Willis, and curiosity about what had happened to him at school was eating at me. I also wanted to know more about the Merrills. I decided to spy on them from my tree house.

When I was in first grade, Daddy had built it for me in the old oak that grew right alongside the fence that separated our yard from the Ogles'. I hadn't used it much last summer, and I hadn't been in it at all this year. The tree house had a back wall and sides just high enough to hold up a roof. The front was wide open, so I would have a good view of our new neighbors. If I slid to the back wall, they wouldn't be able to see me.

I climbed up and heaved myself onto the floor and pulled my legs in. At that moment, Elliot jumped over the fence to get a spade from our shed. When he got back to his own yard, Mrs. Merrill said, "Elliot, your pa won't like it we didn't ask his permission. You know how he is."

"We've got to eat, that's all I know. I doubt Pa will notice a garden. We've been here three days and he hasn't even looked at the other rooms in the house, just the one he eats in and the one he passes out in."

"Elliot!" Mrs. Merrill looked around as if to see if anyone had heard him.

"Look, Carolyn, I hope Pa keeps this job, I really do. But you know that if he keeps the rent paid up, there won't be a whole lot of money left. With a garden, at least we'll have some food."

Rent? It never entered my head to think about how my family paid their bills and if there'd be enough food. It seemed funny to hear those words coming out of Elliot's mouth. Mr. Merrill didn't sound like too good a husband or dad from what they were saying. It made me think back to that time he chased Willis with a belt. Would he really have hit him?

Elliot said, "I'll look for odd jobs around town. We'll have beans and tomato plants. It will be a nice garden. Don't worry about it."

But Mrs. Merrill looked worried, all right. She looked scared to death. She had on a wrinkled green skirt and a matching jacket that looked, well, tired. When it was new, it was the sort of thing you'd wear to get fancied up, and here she was wearing it as a housedress.

My ears perked up when I heard Elliot ask, "How did school go for Willis?"

"Not too good. He brought home a letter from the principal. I think he was upset, but you know Willis—he wouldn't talk about it. He took Zorro out of the cage and ran off." Mrs. Merrill seemed about to cry when she said, "The principal wants one of his parents to come to school."

"Then you'll have to go," Elliot said.

"I can't."

"Then who will? You know Pa won't. You're our stepmother now. You'll have to go tell them how it is with Willis."

How what is? I wanted to scream the question.

"Your pa won't like it. You know how mad he gets when he thinks I butt in with you boys."

Elliot was attacking the garden. "What I *know* is that they won't listen to me because I'm not an adult. Pa won't go, so it'll have to be you."

Big tears welled in Mrs. Merrill's eyes. Elliot said, "Don't even tell Pa about the letter and everything will be fine. Just go on back in the house now."

Then she turned to go! I'd never seen anything like these people. If you didn't know better, you would have thought Elliot was the grownup.

• • •

When Elliot was alone and busy turning over the dirt, I decided this was a good time to find out what had happened to Willis.

"Hey!" I yelled from the treehouse.

Elliot looked around, not seeing me. "Up here!" I called.

"Hey, yourself," Elliot said when he saw me, then went back to work.

I climbed down the ladder and got the hoe out of the shed. Then I hopped the fence and began breaking up the dirt clods that Elliot had turned over. He stopped and looked at me.

"This garden hasn't been used since Mr. Ogle got sick. That was a few years back. It's going to be hard work. I thought it would be neighborly to help."

Elliot watched me for a few more minutes, then finally said, "You don't have to do this. I can manage. But if you want to be 'neighborly,' then I'll say thanks."

Unlike Willis, Elliot seemed okay to me. He was nice but not overly much. He wasn't one of those people who fawned all over you.

Beth must have heard our voices. The back door slammed and she came running out. She stood hopping from her bare tiptoes back to her heels, sucking on that finger. She seemed excited but wouldn't say a word until Elliot looked at her and smiled. Then she said, "Hi!"

I didn't care much for babies or little kids. They seemed like a lot of work. They almost never did what you wanted them to, and they always looked kind of dirty to me. Beth's hair lay in strings, and I wondered if anyone ever washed her face. But it made me sad that she needed Elliot's okay to talk to me.

"Hey, Beth," I said.

Her excitement took over again. She thrust her doll out to me. It had an old rag wrapped around it. "She has clothes now!" she said.

"Well, so she does." I tried to think of something else to say. "Does this well-dressed baby have a name?"

Beth stopped smiling and looked at the ground as if she was thinking real hard. I had the feeling no one had ever really played with her before. I thought of my Ginny and Betsy McCall dolls stuck away in my closet along with a hatbox full of doll clothes. Mother might not be one to show affection, unlike Daddy and Nanna, but she never hesitated to spend money. Every Christmas morning when I was younger, she gave me more doll clothes than any three kids ought to have— according to Nanna.

It tugged at my heart that Beth didn't know dolls should have clothes or names. I said, "We should call her Elizabeth. I've heard only very special babies get that name."

When I said that, she bounced up and down with sheer joy, clutching her doll to her. I was glad Mrs. Merrill had told us that Beth's full name was Elizabeth.

"I'm going to tell Mama her name!" she said, and she ran into the house.

Elliot didn't miss turning a shovel of dirt but he said, "That was a nice thing to say."

I kept working, too, but the ground didn't seem as hard as it had when I started. We worked side by side for a while. When Elliot stopped to wipe his face with his shirtsleeve, I took the chance to talk about Willis. "Your brother is in my class at school."

"Yeah?"

"Yeah. I was surprised you'd sign up for school when it's almost over for the year."

Elliot smiled. "You sound like Willis." Then he got serious. "An education's important. Just look around you. It's the only way poor folks can get a good job."

I acted interested, but Elliot's words reminded me of all the speeches Nanna and Daddy always gave me.

I tried to get the subject back to Willis. "A funny thing happened today. He was in my class only for a while. Then he sort of disappeared."

Elliot went right back to the garden. "That a fact?" he asked.

"Yep." I went back to work, too. "I'm not sure, but I think he might be in trouble. He got sent to the principal's office and we didn't see him again for the entire day."

I didn't think he was going to answer me. Finally he said, "It was probably a mistake putting him in sixth grade. Willis has an awful hard time reading."

"Heck, it's not my favorite thing to do, either. I almost never read a book unless I have to."

"It's not that he doesn't want to. It's that he can't. For some reason the letters just don't make sense to him. Some schools we've gone to put him in with kids his own age. Others bump him down a grade or two. Sounds like that's what'll happen here."

I lived in dread of flunking a grade. Willis was one of the tallest kids in our class. That would make it even worse. But after all I'd been through with Willis, I thought it sounded like good punishment for a bully. Still, I didn't want to show

Elliot my feelings, so I acted as if I felt bad about it. "Being set back a grade or two would be a hard thing."

Elliot cut in fast. "Willis will be all right. He might not read real good, but he'll do okay. It's not like he doesn't have anybody to take care of him. He has me. I'll always be there to look out for him."

Elliot was looking right at me with his blond hair hanging in his eyes. He had the most serious look I'd ever seen.

I felt kind of flustered and said, "Yeah, you're right. There're worse things. He'll be just fine."

I wiped my hands on my pants. "Nanna'll be wondering what happened to me. I ought to go in now."

I jumped back over the fence and ran all the way into the house and didn't stop until I was in my bedroom. Grabbing the pillow off my bed, I wrapped my arms around it. It was the first time since I had learned about Robert that I didn't run for the sock drawer to pull out his picture when I was upset. I carried the pillow over to my window and looked down at Elliot's back as he worked the soil.

There was something about the way he looked when he said, "He has me. I'll always be there to look out for him," that tore right into my heart. With his straight blond hair and bright blue eyes, Elliot didn't look a thing like my picture of Robert. Yet he'd said exactly what I thought Robert would say about me if he had ever had the chance. It was what I pretended he said when I had his picture out.

My heart pounded so hard that I squeezed the pillow tighter to my chest. My throat was tight and my eyes stung.

It didn't seem right that mean Willis Merrill should have a big brother in the here and now when all I had was a brother I couldn't mention around my mother, a brother made up of nothing but an old photograph and borrowed memories.

6

Tuesday morning Willis came to school, but none of us could figure out where he went.

After school he ran out the door as if a demon were on his trail. He must've beat it straight home to get his raccoon, because Zorro's cage was empty when I got there. That suited me just fine. Still, I couldn't help wondering about it.

"Where did Willis take off to?" I asked Elliot when he came over to borrow our gardening tools.

"Willis keeps to himself" was the only answer I got.

Elliot was a hard worker. He was planting the seed potatoes and onion sets Nanna had given him. He said he also planned to grow pole beans, tomatoes, and turnips. After working in his garden, he came over to ours. I could tell that a weed wouldn't stand a chance with Elliot around.

I'd noticed that Elliot and Willis walked to school together. Willis hurried home, though, and Elliot came home alone. Since he didn't have a bike, I stopped riding mine to school—waiting to leave the house until after Willis and Elliot were a block ahead of me. Lord knows, I didn't want to walk to school with Willis! Then I only had to dawdle a little

after school before Elliot came by and we walked home together.

Wednesday afternoon, I was walking with Elliot when
chubby Bobby Wayans saw us and yelled, "Ooh, Lydia's got a
boyfriend! I wonder if he knows she's mean as a hornet?"

I spun around to say something, but Elliot put his arm on
mine to still me. He turned to Bobby and said, "Excuse me?
Do you have something to say to me?"

Bobby swallowed hard. "Um, no," he mumbled.

"Do you have something to say to Lydia?" Elliot asked.

Bobby hung his head and said, "No."

"Good. Let's keep it that way," Elliot said as we walked
away. It was exactly the kind of thing a big brother should say
to defend you. I don't think my feet touched the sidewalk all
the way home.

Life seemed just fine as it was. School was almost out for
the year, I was making a friend in Elliot, and Willis hadn't
been in my class since Monday. I should have let Willis's being
so mean to me roll off me like water off a duck's back. But I
couldn't. I wanted to get even with him. It didn't seem right
that he should get off scot-free.

Zorro was his weak spot, so that's what I zeroed in on.
When I got home, I changed out of my school clothes and
pedaled my bike to the one place I never went unless I had
to—the library. I walked straight to the card catalog and
looked up the word "raccoon." I found what I needed in the
reference section.

"Raccoons!" Mrs. Green said when she saw my book. "So
you're going to make friends with that new boy. Well, you're
on the right track. If he has a pet raccoon, then you need

to find out all you can about them. That will impress him."

She gave my book a loud *tha-wump!* with the date stamp, closed it with a bang, and handed it to me as she winked. "Always pretend to care about a boy's interests. That's how I got my Sam."

I smiled a shaky smile and almost ran out of there before anybody saw me. With that loud voice of hers, even the mice in the library basement could have heard Mrs. Green.

I spent all my free time that night and the next day reading about raccoons. I read that they can be mischievous. I read that they are more active at night than in the daytime. I read and read and then I stopped reading when I got to the part about how much they love certain foods. That's when I knew what to do.

Nanna kept our pantry stocked with food in case a natural disaster left us stranded. She was prepared—never mind that we were just a few blocks from the grocery store. I searched through the shelves until my eyes landed on a jar of peanut butter. It was perfect. I hid it behind the boxwood bush beneath my bedroom window.

Near as I could tell, the only way to get to Zorro without Willis would be in the morning before Willis woke up. Nanna got up at six, so that meant I'd have to get up at five o'clock.

That night I put a pillow over my alarm clock so it wouldn't wake the house. When its vibration woke me on Friday, I hurried and put on my jeans and a sweater. I stuck a pencil in my pocket, then opened my bedroom window. It wasn't easy to climb out, but I thought of Robert climbing the water tower and that's all the courage I needed.

I landed on the ground and grabbed the peanut butter jar. Then I sneaked over the fence and tiptoed to Zorro's cage. I opened the jar and put a dab of peanut butter on the end of the pencil. I stuck it in the cage and let him eat it off the pencil. Then I unlatched his cage and left a trail of peanut butter right up to the oak tree that had my tree house in it. Reaching as high as I could where the tree leaned over the fence into the Merrills' yard, I ground a little of it into the bark. Then I went back over the fence into my yard, climbed into my tree house, and waited.

Zorro ate the bits of peanut butter on the trail, then scampered up the tree. He hesitated where he smelled the ground-in peanut butter, then ran right up to the tree house. I planned to ease my way to the ground and leave another trail back to his cage, but as soon as I started down that tree, Zorro was right after me. I jumped the fence and ran to his cage with him on my heels. I threw a blob of peanut butter inside his cage, and as soon as he went in, I locked it.

Zorro had caught on fast. I would just have to unlock his cage and then run to my tree house to have him follow. Now I would wait for the right moment to trick Willis into thinking that Zorro liked me more than him.

The second Free Show came and went. It wasn't near as eventful as the first one. I knew there was no way Rae Anne could talk her folks into coming two weeks in a row, but not having her there was still a letdown. I'd dreaded seeing Willis, but he didn't show up. Neither did Elliot, another disappointment. To top it off, the movie didn't start until twenty minutes after dark, so I spent a long night listening to Nanna complain and having no friend to share it with. The only good thing about the show was the serial. Last week we had seen the first ten minutes of *Buck Rogers* and then the movie. This week we saw the next ten minutes. I liked the serial more than the movie, although *Singin' in the Rain* wasn't bad.

Saturday morning I found Nanna taking clothes down from the clothesline. I knew she was using it as an excuse to talk to Mrs. Merrill, since taking down the laundry was my job. I sneaked out the back porch and crouched in my hiding place behind the steps so I could listen.

"I do laundry every Monday and Thursday, and I do sheets on Saturday. You can use the clothesline on Tuesdays, Wednesdays, or Fridays."

"Oh, I don't know. I get along all right without one," Mrs. Merrill said, not meeting Nanna's eye.

"You'd have one if Violet Ogle hadn't been so proud of her fancy umbrella-style clothesline and taken it with her." Nanna snapped the last pillowcase in the air. "A person can do without a fancy washing machine. All they need is water, soap, and elbow grease. But there's nothing like the smell of clothes after the sun's warmed them, is there? And there's no sense in your husband putting up a clothesline when I have a perfectly good one right here."

Folding the pillowcase, Nanna placed it on top of the basket. Then she took off her apron and handed it to Mrs. Merrill. "Here you go. The clothespins are in the pocket. You might as well go ahead and use it tomorrow. I never do wash on Sunday. After you take your clothes down, just hang the apron on a peg on my back porch."

Nanna gave her a huge smile as if it had all been settled.

Mrs. Merrill finally gave in and reached for the apron. She looked beaten. Nanna could do that to a person.

Then, without looking my way, Nanna said, "Lydia, you can bring the clothes basket in now," and walked right past me into the kitchen. Nanna always told me she had eyes in the back of her head. I had every reason to believe her.

I lugged that clothes basket into the kitchen and dropped it with a thud. "I don't know why you offered them our clothesline," I said to Nanna. "She's had that same sorry green dress on since she moved in. It's probably so dirty it could stand up by itself."

Crack! Nanna brought a wooden spoon down hard on the counter. "Lydia Carson, you shame me. How is she supposed to clean their clothes? She has no washing machine and probably no money for the Laundromat. Sometimes folks just need a helping hand. That's a lesson you should remember."

"Yes'm," I said, but mostly I thought the lesson I'd remember was not to get too sassy while Nanna had a wooden spoon within reach.

That night the grown-ups had coffee on our front porch after supper. Since I didn't have anything better to do, I sat with them.

Suddenly Mr. Merrill's truck came screeching around the corner. He pulled up in front of his house a little too fast and parked the truck with its front wheel in the grass. He got out, staggered, and then walked a little unsteadily into the house.

"Why, he's drunk!" Nanna said.

"It does look like it," Daddy answered.

"Land sakes, no wonder Carolyn acts scared all the time."

"And what, pray tell, does this have to do with us?" Mother asked.

"Oh, nothing. I've just been wondering why Carolyn acts so peculiar. This explains it."

"Coming home a little drunk one night doesn't make him an alcoholic," Mother said. "Maybe Carolyn is peculiar all by herself."

"I don't think so . . ." Nanna murmured as she stared at the Merrills' house. Nanna had that look she got when she couldn't keep her nose out of other people's business. I could tell by Mother's face that she saw it, too.

I didn't want to hear them bickering, so I went into the kitchen. I reached for the handle on the Frigidaire and tried not to look at the door. Nanna had stuck the church bulletin on with a magnet. She'd circled the date of the mother-daughter banquet in bright red: Sunday, May 27. That was tomorrow. I cringed every time I saw that bulletin. It did a better job of keeping me out of the refrigerator than Nanna's "You'll spoil your supper" ever did.

I dreaded the banquet. I might have looked forward to it if Mother had wanted me to go, but the celebration was all for Nanna. It made me feel that Mother and I were both Nanna's daughters and reminded me of how distant Mother and I were.

Nanna and Mother brought their coffee cups into the kitchen while I sat there brooding about the banquet. When Nanna asked what dress I wanted to wear to it, the words exploded from my mouth. "Oh, Nanna, why do I have to go? Mother's going. Isn't one daughter enough for you? Do you have to have two?"

Mother got that steely look in her eyes. "You don't have to go to the banquet."

"What?" Nanna looked shocked.

"It *is* a mother-daughter banquet, is it not? Lydia is *my* daughter. I do have these facts straight, don't I?" she asked Nanna.

"Well, yes, but—"

"Fine. I'm telling her she can skip it."

I looked from Mother to Nanna. I didn't feel good that I'd pitted them against each other. Still, I didn't have to go, so I can't say I felt *all* bad.

When Mother and Nanna headed for the banquet Sunday evening, Daddy said, "It's not every day I get to have supper with a beautiful girl. How about you and I go to the Oasis tonight?"

"Great!"

And it was great. I even got a root beer float with my supper. As we walked back to the house, Daddy said, "That grass is so tall I'll have to either mow it tonight or bale it. What are you going to do, girl?"

"Just take out the trash, I guess."

"I'll do that. I don't like you being around that burn barrel."

Everyone in Maywood had a barrel for burning their trash. While Daddy was outside lighting the fire, the phone rang. Someone had a flat tire and needed Daddy to open up the station and patch it.

"I'm sorry but duty calls, Ladybug." Daddy gave me a crooked smile. "Will you be all right here, or do you want to come along?"

68

Then it hit me. With everyone gone, this would be a perfect time to play my little trick on Willis. "I'll be fine, Daddy. I'll mosey over if I get bored."

After Daddy left, I sat on the back porch until I heard that clicking noise that could only be Zorro. I climbed up my tree house with the jar of peanut butter.

I had a clear view of Willis with Zorro on his back. I opened the peanut butter jar and, sure enough, Zorro leaped off Willis's back and came at a dead run to my tree house. Oh, it was as beautiful as any ballet. He ran up the side of the tree and sat next to me to get that peanut butter, just the way we'd practiced.

I took special pleasure in watching the expressions cross Willis's face. There were so many of them! Then he started that clicking sound he made to call Zorro—which Zorro ignored. From the ground Willis couldn't see I was feeding his raccoon.

"Well, ain't that a hoot! Looks like Zorro's my new friend," I said. Then I talked baby talk to Zorro. "Isn't that right, Zorro? We're friends, aren't we?"

"You— What the—" Willis sputtered. I remembered when Willis got mad at the Free Show what a hard time he'd had finding words. It was as if they flew right out of his head and left him sputtering. Now he was doing it again.

We heard a bang as Beth ran out the screen door. "Hi, Lydia! Willis, look! Zorro is with Lydia!" She raised her doll's hand and said, "Wave to Zorro and Lydia, Elizabeth!"

The other thing I remembered about Willis was how cruel he could be when he was mad.

Beth was standing next to Willis. She smiled and waved her doll's arm. Willis turned to her.

My brain registered that she was too close to him. That she should run. But my mouth wasn't able to form the words fast enough.

In his white-hot anger, Willis reached out. He grabbed the first thing his hand landed on. He yanked Elizabeth out of Beth's arms and flung the doll away. It landed in the burn barrel.

Almost immediately Elizabeth's face caved in on itself and her hair burst into flames. I don't remember climbing out of that tree, but there I was, holding Beth's tiny, shaking body so she couldn't see her only toy in the world burning up.

I knew as I held her that it wasn't just Willis's fault. If I hadn't goaded him, he wouldn't have gotten so mad. I would have shared the blame with him, but he didn't stay long enough to apologize. He ran like the chickenhearted goon that he was.

When Beth's shaking sobs stopped, I said to her, "I'll be right back."

I tore through my closet, my tears making everything look wobbly. I yanked down the hatbox from my closet shelf. Inside I found my Betsy McCall and Ginny dolls and a pile of doll clothes.

I picked out a crocheted white dress with red tatting because it was the prettiest doll dress I had, a green satin traveling suit because it was probably what Mrs. Merrill's sad jacket and skirt had looked like new, and a frilly pink bridesmaid dress with a matching veil and a little bouquet of plastic flowers. I threw them all into an old Buster Brown shoebox and laid Betsy McCall on top. Ginny was my favorite, with glossy brown hair and eyes, but I knew Betsy was the doll that was needed today. I was halfway down the stairs when I really looked at the Buster Brown shoebox. It looked so plain, so . . . used.

I ran back upstairs and dumped everything out of a beautiful carved wooden chest that sat on my dresser and put the clothes and doll in it. She looked real pretty in the chest.

Beth wasn't outside, so I went around front. I was relieved to see Mr. Merrill and Elliot climb into the truck and pull away. Mr. Merrill didn't sit right with me and I didn't want to go there when he was home. I knocked on the Merrills' door.

When Mrs. Merrill answered, I said, "Hello, Miz Merrill. Could Beth come outside?"

Mrs. Merrill looked as if she'd been crying, too. "Beth isn't feeling well right now, Lydia. Maybe you should come back tomorrow."

"Miz Merrill, I know about her doll. I'd really like to see her."

Beth's little face peeked around her mama's skirt.

"Do you want to see Lydia, honey?"

Beth nodded and came outside. She sat on the porch step. I waited until Mrs. Merrill went back inside.

"Hey, Beth," I said gently, sitting beside her. "I'm so glad to see you. I have someone I'd like you to meet."

Beth's pale face was streaked from crying. When she saw that carved chest, her eyes grew twice their size.

I carefully set the box down between us, lifted the lid, and took out the doll. "Isn't she pretty?"

Beth nodded.

"She has such nice clothes to wear. Just look at this beautiful jacket and skirt."

"It looks like Mama's!" Beth said.

"Well, what do you know? It sure does! Would you like to hold her?"

Beth nodded and I laid the doll in her arms. She held it carefully, like a real baby.

"There's a sad story about this doll. She doesn't have anybody who wants to play with her anymore. There's nothing sadder than a doll that has to stay by herself in a box all day long." I stared off into space for a minute to let the words soak in.

"I was wondering if maybe you'd like to play with her."

Beth's face lit up and she nodded hard.

"There's only one catch. If she gets used to playing with you, she'll be just miserable if she has to play with anybody else. That kind of means you'd have to keep her forever. Think you could do that?"

"Ohhh. Yes!"

"Whew, that's a relief. I think she'll really like being your forever doll. Did I tell you her name?"

"No."

"It's Betsy McCall."

"Betsy," Beth said as she looked at her.

"I like that name Betsy. Have you ever heard it before?"

"Uh-huh."

"Did you know that Betsy is another nickname for Elizabeth, like Beth?"

Beth looked at me with a face that showed so much love and joy that I just wanted to die. I hadn't thrown her doll into the fire. And I couldn't have known things would get so out of hand. But the sick feeling in the pit of my stomach reminded me that Willis had done it because of me.

7

There's a saying in Indiana that if you don't like the weather, stick around: it'll change. The night Beth's doll burned, the heat gave way to a cold snap and driving rain.

On Monday, school was a little more bearable with the stickiness gone, but the rain meant indoor recess, which was darn near intolerable. We sat in huddles, trading theories about what became of Willis every school day. I remembered Elliot saying that some schools held him back a year or two, but we saw the fourth and fifth graders playing at recess. Willis wasn't among them.

We saw him come to school, but the front door was like a mouth that swallowed him whole.

The rain would keep Elliot out of the gardens, but I'd brought an umbrella with me so we could still walk home together. Being taller, he held the umbrella up over me. The rain washed down around us as if we were in our own little cocoon, and I never wanted that walk to end.

I couldn't get up the courage to ask Elliot about Willis again.

Nosy Bobby Wayans tried his best to find out, though. He said he hung around the lunchroom on Monday, thinking Willis *had* to eat, but never saw him. So Tuesday, Bobby came to school early and skulked by the front door. Willis marched right by, even though Bobby called out to him, and went straight to the school office.

Wednesday was Memorial Day, a national holiday. I knew it was supposed to be a somber day, spent decorating the graves of soldiers and other loved ones who had passed on. But how could it be somber when it meant no school?

Nanna let me sleep in, probably because Mother was home and was always real quiet on that day. We knew it was because Robert's grave was in Ohio and too far away for her to visit, but no one ever said a word about that.

Daddy, Nanna, and I took fresh flowers to the graves of Daddy's parents, who'd died before I was born. Then Daddy took Mother for a long drive. He called it a special "date," but Nanna and I knew he was just trying to cheer her up.

The day after Memorial Day, May 31, was the last day of school. Hallelujah! And it wasn't a real school day. We went just in the morning to clean out our desks and to pick up our report cards. Mrs. Warren passed them out, telling us how much she had enjoyed having us and how she would miss us. She didn't fool us one bit: we knew she was tickled pink to be rid of us.

I slowly slid my report card out of its manila envelope. At the bottom I found the word I was looking for: "promoted," as in promoted to seventh grade. I knew my grades were good enough, but I never rested easy until I saw that word at the bottom of the year's last report card.

Willis didn't come to school that day, but Mrs. Merrill finally did, holding tight to Beth's hand. I remembered what she'd said to Elliot and wondered if her husband knew she was there. It made me wonder if there was a little more pluck to her than I'd thought.

"Can I help you, Mrs. Merrill?" I said.

"I just need to see the principal, but thank you for offering." She said it politely, but I noticed she squeezed Beth's hand harder when she went to the office.

It ended up being Junior Plunkett who solved the mystery of where Willis had been since his first day in our school. Junior was the son of the school nurse, who liked to think she had her finger on the pulse of the school. She was also a blabbermouth, and Junior soaked up everything she said like a sponge.

After we got our report cards, we all gathered in front of the school for our official class portrait, then went inside to collect anything worth saving from our desks before going home. On the way back in, Junior said, "That new kid was in the principal's office all of last week. They were doing tests to figure out where to stick him." Then he shut up with a smug look, waiting for us to beg him to finish.

Bobby gave in right away. "Aw, come on, Junior. Tell us."

"What's it worth to you?"

"Either tell us or don't," I snapped.

"Well," Junior puffed up as if he had some big FBI secret. "They were gonna keep him back a year, then two. Then he went and did something that only a crazy person would do." He paused for effect. "He spit in the principal's face."

We all gasped.

"It's true as I'm standing here."

He was right. Only a crazy person would spit in the principal's face.

"So," Junior continued, "they decided to put him in Special Ed! That's where he's been this week."

"Nah," Bobby said. "We'd have seen him."

"You know they don't allow the Special Ed kids to eat in the cafeteria or have recess with the rest of us," Junior said.

Special Ed was the room on the top floor of the school near the back. When you walked by, you'd see one kid sitting in a chair drooling and another walking around a circular table, again and again. Whenever I saw that boy, I always wondered which class was directly beneath him, because one of these days he'd wear a hole clean through, and he and the table would both come crashing down on a round disk of floor.

"Special Ed?" We whispered those dreaded words to each other. It wasn't an option any of us had considered. Willis was mean and headstrong, but he didn't drool. He seemed to carry on like a normal human being. Mostly. A mean normal human being.

You could see the air going out of Bobby. His new friend, his ticket to the other boys' games at recess, had just been snatched beyond his reach. Whether it was right or wrong, the truth was nobody wanted a friend in Special Ed.

Then something wonderful dawned on me: Next year I'd be in seventh grade, and grades seven through twelve went to the high school. Special Ed kids stayed in the grade school, no matter what their age. Willis wouldn't be in my class anymore. He wouldn't even be in my school. Bobby Wayans was crushed. To top it off, this was the last day of school for the summer.

All in all, it made for a perfect day.

Friday night, Daddy shoveled peas into his mouth as fast as he could. "I'm sorry I can't walk you ladies to the Free Show, but I promised Sam I'd—"

"Help with the projector. Yes, dear. You mentioned it several times."

It made my stomach ache when Mother talked to Daddy like that. I looked up and knew that even she saw the hurt on his face.

"It's only a few blocks to the library. We'll be fine," she said in a softer tone.

"What's the movie tonight, Daddy?" I said.

"*Ma and Pa Kettle at the Fair.*"

"Great!" I smiled real big, hoping to cheer him.

He patted me on the shoulder. "Well, then, I'd best be getting along."

Daddy and Sam had spent the better part of the week rounding up an old chicken coop to act as a projection room for the Free Show. They'd hauled it to the library yard, and everything would have been fine if it hadn't been for another downpour. Now Daddy was worried about the chicken coop not being stable enough and wanted to get to the library early to help.

"Glen only worries out of love, Evelyn," Nanna said after he left.

"Too much worrying can feel like suffocation whether it's done in the name of love or not," Mother said right back.

Nanna gave a big sigh. She began stacking the dishes and said, "I've been thinking and I just don't know if I should go tonight. I don't think these old bones of mine can sit on the hard ground another time. Besides, it's bound to be damp and I visit Louise in just a week and a half. It'd disappoint her so if I caught a cold and couldn't go."

"You don't have to go to the show, Nanna," I said as I

helped her clear the table. "Daddy said not many folks would be there tonight because of the rain."

Nanna let out another sigh. "Glen said they'd have benches by now. I realize the rain slowed the work down, but—"

"It isn't just the rain, you know," Mother said. "The other merchants want the shows, but they don't want to do any of the labor. It's all up to Sam and Glen, and there's only so much two men can do."

"I know," Nanna said. "Still, you'd think they'd give those benches priority."

I threw back my head and stared at the light fixture. I wondered what would happen if I bumped Nanna the way I bumped my record player when it got stuck. Would she start talking about something else?

Mother rolled her eyes and said, "Nanna, I have an idea. Why don't you stay here tonight? Glen promised there would be benches set up, but the rain ruined that plan. I don't think you should sit on the hard ground, especially since it's bound to be damp."

"I think you're right, Evelyn. I think I'll stay home."

I pretended to have a coughing fit in order to stifle a laugh.

"We should get started," Mother said.

So Mother and I would be alone. I couldn't remember the last time we had done anything together, just us two. I felt kind of fluttery and happy inside.

When we were in the hall, she whispered to me, "Grab a couple of folding chairs, but don't let Nanna see you. If she realizes she has the option of not sitting on the ground, she'll come up with a new set of worries we'll be forced to endure."

"Yes'm," I said, smiling. I knew it was mean-spirited of me

to get such a kick out of Mother saying unkind things about Nanna, but some of Nanna's ways sure got tiresome.

Mother stuck a pencil behind her ear and a pad of paper in her pocket in case there was some breaking news she could write a story about. She never went anywhere without them. Other than that, I felt as if we were just any mother and daughter.

I studied her out of the corner of my eye. She looked straight ahead but didn't have that faraway look she had most of the time. I cleared my throat and took a chance that she might be in a talkative mood.

"That was pretty good the way you got around Nanna. She'd still be there yammering about not wanting to come if you hadn't said something."

"I've had a lifetime of practice," she said drily.

"Sometimes I forget that Nanna raised you, too. I mean— that she's helping to raise me," I stammered.

"Yes, I never dreamed that Nanna would still be giving orders and running the household when I reached the ripe old age that I have."

"You're not old, Mother."

"Don't kid yourself, Lydia. Most of your friends have grandmothers my age."

It was kind of true, with her being almost fifty, but it was also something I didn't like thinking about.

"Well, Daddy's younger. He's more the age of the other dads."

"Thank you for reminding me," she said in that way she had that made me feel I couldn't say one blessed thing right.

"I mean—"

"I know what you mean, Lydia. And here we are! Hello, Beverly!" Mother set down her chair and was off talking to Mrs. Green.

Just one time I wanted to talk to Mother without messing up. I wanted to say something interesting enough to make her come toward me instead of skittering away. I put my chair next to hers and flopped down in it. I knew she wouldn't sit in that chair until it was too dark to do anything else.

I decided to take a walk up Main Street to see if I could find someone I knew. There was a little crowd lined up in front of the Oasis Café. Elliot was there, wearing a chef's apron and holding a box with a few bags of popcorn in it. Pure happiness washed over me when I saw him. He was all cleaned up, his hair parted on the side and combed. He looked real nice.

"Hey, Elliot."

"Hey, Lydia."

His smile gave me the courage to walk around the crowd and stand beside him. "Do they know you're taking away their business at the Oasis?" I asked.

"Taking it away? They gave me the job. See?" He tilted his box so I could read the lettering on the front. It had a Coca-Cola advertisement on it and THE OASIS printed underneath.

"Is this job for all summer or just tonight?"

"I'll be working at the café all summer as a busboy. I'll sell popcorn at the Free Shows for as long as it works, I guess. The plan is, people will get thirsty from the popcorn and come to the restaurant for a drink."

"That sounds like a good plan. You come up with it?"

He looked shy and said, "Yeah, how'd you know?"

I put both my hands on the window of the restaurant and

made a show of looking in. "Well, let's see. Big Joe's cooking tonight. I can see his cigarette ashes falling onto the grill. Makes the burgers tasty, don't you know."

Elliot laughed, so I went on. "And Hazel's waiting tables. She must not have had to work the lunch shift, too, or she'd have switched from her clunky white shoes to her house slippers. You know, the ones that flap her feet every time she takes a step."

I came back to Elliot's side. "It had to be your idea. There's nobody else there smart enough to think of it."

Elliot grinned. "Well, we all come out ahead. I get a nickel for each bag of popcorn I sell. They get the rest of the money plus customers coming in for a Coke."

I said, "You're getting low on popcorn. Tell me what to do and I'll help."

He looked uncomfortable. "I'll take care of it."

"No, really, I've got nothing to do. At least till the show starts. I'll run in and bag up popcorn, or I'll sell the bags while you do it."

Elliot looked at me in that straight-in-the-eye way he had and said, "I appreciate the offer, but I can't pay you."

"The chain keeps slipping on my bike. I was hoping you could fix it." Even if that had been true, Daddy would have fixed it for me. Still, it was worth a little lie when Elliot gave me his big smile and said, "Charge them fifteen cents a bag. I'll go make a new batch."

I took the box of popcorn from him and felt that happiness all over again. Funny how just holding a box that Elliot had held could make me feel special.

I was down to the last two bags when Junior Plunkett was

next in line. I had been in such a good mood these past two days, and I knew that Junior's news about Willis had a lot to do with it. For a minute I forgot that I didn't even like Junior all that much.

"One bag, please," he said and held out a dime and nickel.

I handed Junior a bag of popcorn. "This one's on me," I said, reaching into my pocket for the money.

"Thanks!" Then he squinted his eyes. "Is this a trick?"

"No trick. Anyone who gives me good news like you did deserves a treat, that's all."

"Good news? You mean about that new kid?"

"Yeah. Now that they put Willis in Special Ed, he won't even be in the same school as me next year. What better news could I get?"

Junior still looked wary. "If it isn't a trick, what's that kid looking at us so funny for?"

I glanced over my shoulder and there stood Elliot, holding a box full of popcorn bags, looking as if he'd been sucker punched.

8

Elliot had only one thing to say to me. He walked over, took the popcorn box out of my hands, and said, "I don't need your help anymore."

He didn't even look at me when he said it. And I knew he meant more than help with the popcorn. He meant he didn't need me at all.

I wanted to talk to him afterward, to explain myself, but no words I came up with were good enough. I'd never once let on to Elliot how much I hated Willis.

On Sunday morning, Nanna, Daddy, and I headed out for church. Nanna spotted Mrs. Merrill on her front porch and invited her to come with us. Mrs. Merrill said no. Maybe she and God had "parted ways," too. Otherwise I hadn't laid eyes on a Merrill all weekend.

I spent that afternoon shut up in my room with Robert's picture. I told him that I hadn't meant to hurt Elliot, that it wasn't my fault Willis was so darned mean. No matter how much I talked, though, I didn't feel any better.

Come Monday morning, Nanna put me to work hanging the clothes on the line. It's funny how during school you count the days till summer, thinking the fun is going to start with a big blast—like the best fireworks on the Fourth of July, the ones that look like the biggest carnation filling up the sky and making everybody say "Ahhhh." Then there are you, first day of summer vacation, picking up soggy shirts and clipping them to the clothesline.

After we ate a quick lunch, Nanna said, "Grab some berry baskets off the back porch and meet me around front. We have work to do."

Nanna marched up to the Merrills' front door. I lagged behind with the baskets. I didn't want to see Willis's mean face or Elliot's accusing one.

"How do, Carolyn! Isn't it a lovely day?"

"Hello, Nanna."

"Lydia and I were just on our way to the old Pearson place. It's vacant now, but there is a patch of wild strawberries growing that's just begging for someone to come pick it. Lydia will keep an eye on Beth for you, and tonight you and I will be serving fresh strawberries for dessert. Won't that be fine?"

Mrs. Merrill looked plumb exhausted. It's no wonder, the way Nanna had been badgering her about a garden, then the clothesline, and now strawberry picking.

"Nanna, I really don't think I—"

"Carolyn, I'm not taking no for an answer. I can't pick like I used to or I'd pick enough to give you, and I can't stand to think of those berries going to waste. Now, you and Beth get ready."

She marched back down the steps and said, "I'm bringing the car around."

I perked up and watched her open the garage door. She got behind the wheel of our 1957 Chevy Belair as if it were the most natural thing in the world. I couldn't remember the last time Nanna had driven. She acted as if the price of gas would put us in the poorhouse, which was funny, considering Daddy owned a gas station. So it was odd seeing her whip the car out of the garage. I said a quick prayer to our Maker that she remembered how to drive the danged thing.

Beth and I sat in the back with Betsy McCall in the wooden box between us. It annoyed me that she had to take the box with her. She didn't know how to play at all. What if I'd given her, say, a pogo stick? Would she have brought that along, too?

"You know, you don't need to bring Betsy's box every-where. You can leave it at home."

"Oh, no! It's mine. I have to keep it with me." She put her arm around the box. Then I realized she was probably afraid of what Willis would do if she left it at home.

Once we were out on the road, Mrs. Merrill really opened up. She seemed happy to have someone to talk to.

"It's true, I was young when I had Beth," she said to Nanna. Then she turned back and smiled at Beth. Lowering her voice, she added, "Her daddy, her *real* daddy, that is, took off before she was even born. There I was, back in my father's house with a baby in tow. After I'd sworn I'd never go back, too."

"Well, we've all made promises to ourselves and had to break them," Nanna said.

"Daddy acted like he hated it, but I think it gave his life purpose, ranting and raving at me about my poor choice of a husband and all. It sounds silly, but he never seemed happy unless he had someone to yell at, and my mamma had passed on, so there was just me at home." She kind of giggled. "I guess you could say I made him a very happy man, in a round-about way."

She and Nanna laughed.

"I always wanted to be a beautician." She said it almost shyly.

"You do have a knack for hair. I always notice how beauti-ful your hair looks," Nanna told her.

Mrs. Merrill turned her face away, but I could see she was pleased.

"Well, it doesn't really matter now. Do you know it costs

two hundred and fifty dollars at the Beauty Academy in Louisville, Kentucky, to get your beautician's license?"

"Do tell!"

"Yes, ma'am. Two hundred and fifty dollars. I was trying to save the money. We lived in a small town in Kentucky where everybody knew everybody's business. I thought Beth and I could start over in a big city like Louisville where no one knew us. But it might as well have been two thousand dollars."

She tilted her head out the car window to let the air cool her face.

"I'd just come to the conclusion there was no way I could save that much money when along came Boyd Merrill. He wanted to get married. He wanted a mother for his boys. My father said if I married Boyd there was no coming back this time. Beth and I had to sneak out through my bedroom window with just the clothes on our backs! But I did it mainly because I'd always felt bad about Beth not having a daddy, so . . . here we are."

That explained Mrs. Merrill's one dress. I wondered if she'd have been so quick to climb out that window if she'd known Willis was part of the bargain.

Beth was drifting off to sleep. I moved the box to the floor and gently leaned her toward me. Her eyes fluttered, then she put her head down on my leg. I turned my attention back to Nanna and Mrs. Merrill, but Nanna was looking at me in her rearview mirror. She squared her shoulder and asked, "Have you driven over to Aylesville yet?"

Shoot! She probably changed the subject so I wouldn't hear the good stuff.

"No, Boyd's job keeps him away so much."

"Really? What does he do?"

"Boyd's friend used to work at the McMillan factory. When he quit, Boyd applied for his job and we moved here," Mrs. Merrill said. "Boyd says it's hot as Hades in that factory. He works lots of hours and it tires him out. When he's home, he doesn't like to go anywhere."

"Well, that's Boyd's excuse. What about you? Have you driven over?"

"Oh, mercy, no! I can't drive!"

"We'll have to remedy that. A woman never knows when she might need to drive. Your husband could get sick or something and where would you be?"

"Elliot is almost fifteen. He'll be driving soon enough. I don't need to learn how," Mrs. Merrill said with her nervous laugh.

Nanna wasn't laughing at all. "Nonsense. We'll have you driving today."

Beth sat in the shade of the Pearsons' old porch playing with Betsy McCall. Nanna had Mrs. Merrill behind the wheel of the car. They were using the lane to the barn as a road so Nanna could teach her to drive. And me, I stood in the scorching sun picking enough strawberries for two families. Somehow I think that was Nanna's plan all along.

Mrs. Merrill was adamant that Beth not see her driving. "She's too young to keep quiet about this and I can't let Boyd know. He doesn't approve of women driving."

For once Nanna listened. Besides telling me to pick berries, she said to keep Beth around the front of the house.

I could hear the gears grinding. When I was sure Beth was

busy playing, I sneaked around the corner and watched for a bit. I could see the car hop once and die. Then grind-hop-die, all over again. Nanna had been jerked so much in the car that her hair was falling down from its pins, and Mrs. Merrill seemed to be past the point of crying.

Mrs. Merrill stopped the car, got out, and slammed the door. Nanna got out, too. Mrs. Merrill stomped around for a minute, then kicked the car's tire. "Maybe some people just can't drive! Maybe I'm one of them! It's not like I *asked* you for driving lessons, Nanna!"

Nanna went around to the back of the car. Her crown of braids had come completely loose and she sure was a sight.

"Carolyn, you listen to me. I may have forced you into these driving lessons, but if you give up today, you'll regret it for the rest of your life. If there's one thing I can't stand, it's missed opportunities."

She pulled a basket out of the trunk of the car, reached inside, and took out a mason jar of ice tea. She handed it to Mrs. Merrill. While Mrs. Merrill drank, Nanna took a stick and drew in the dust.

"This is the layout of the gears, Carolyn. If you don't start out in first gear, it's going to die on you."

I wanted to hear more but went back to check on Beth. I picked up the full berry baskets, set them on the porch, and said, "I'll be right back, okay, Beth? I need to see if we brought more baskets."

Beth was busy with her doll and just murmured, "Mm-hmm."

When I went back, I heard Nanna say, "Then ease off the clutch at the same time you push the accelerator. When it's done right, it feels just as smooth as a bird gliding across the open sky."

Mrs. Merrill screwed the lid back on her jar and said, "And when it's done wrong, it feels like there's a fool behind the wheel who bit off more than she can chew."

Nanna seemed to consider that for a minute. "Maybe you're right, Carolyn. Maybe you just don't have what it takes."

Nanna saw me and carried two jars of tea over. "Here, Lydia, one for you and one for Beth. And you stay around front with that child, young lady."

"Yes, ma'am."

I walked toward the front of the house, but when I glanced back, Mrs. Merrill was in the driver's seat with a look on her face that said she was going to do this or die trying. Maybe Nanna's stubbornness was rubbing off on her.

I sat on the porch beside Beth and opened her jar of tea. I gulped mine down. Wiping my mouth with the back of my hand, I said, "You've been awful patient, Beth. Have you and Betsy had a good time?"

Beth said, "Shhh. Betsy just got all her babies to sleep."

I looked down and saw six little concoctions made out of hollyhocks. I reached for one and Beth slapped my hand away like a stern little mother.

"I *told* you. The babies are asleep!"

"Oh! These are the babies. I see."

I tried again: "It looks to me like this one is stirring. Mind if I rock her?"

Beth scrunched up her little forehead like a person thinking real hard, then said, "Okay. But just the one."

I picked it up and turned it over in my hand. Someone had

taken a full hollyhock blossom and run a toothpick through
the center of it, then turned it upside down so the petals looked
like a skirt. There was a Hollyhock bud stuck on top of the
toothpick, which was supposed to be the baby's head, and a
second toothpick stuck crossways through the petals to look
like arms.

"Did you make these, Beth?"

"No," she said, fussing with her "babies."

"Did your mama make them? Or Elliot?" I could picture
Elliot doing something like this.

"Willis made them." Beth covered them up with leaves for
blankets and said, "He feels bad about Elizabeth. He makes
me new babies every day."

Willis?

When we got back to the house, Nanna stopped in front to
let Mrs. Merrill and Beth out. She said, "You'd best get out
now, too, Lydia. You know what a tight fit the car is in the
garage."

"Okay. Do you mind if I take a ride on my bike?"

"Run along and enjoy the rest of the afternoon, honey.
You've worked hard today."

I rode straight to the filling station. Daddy had his arm
stretched across a windshield, giving it a good wash, when he
saw me. "Ladybug! It's been so long since you've visited me, I
thought the grass was gonna dry up and blow away."

I felt bad because I hadn't been there since I met Elliot.

"Hi, Daddy."

He finished with the car and said, "We'd best go check out
that pop cooler."

I let the coolness of the Choc-ola wash over my throat, savoring the taste. Then I wiped my mouth and followed Daddy into the front bay, where he had a car on the hoist.

"Daddy, I have a favor to ask."

"A favor? Well, I'll have to check. I might be fresh out of favors."

"I'm serious, Daddy. I want to know if you can loosen my bike chain."

He stopped tinkering with the car and looked at me. "Why?"

"Well, I'd rather not say."

"It's a secret, huh?" He chuckled. "You know if I add a link to your chain, you're going to be right back here wanting me to take the extra link out, don't ya?"

"Maybe."

"Then you'll need another favor, and I already told you I'm running low on them."

I laughed. I figured it was the least I could do.

After he loosened my chain, I pushed my bike all the way home. I was a little out of breath, but I didn't mind—since I planned to talk to Elliot, I thought that might help to cover up my nervousness.

The weather was clear, so he was back in his garden. When I pushed my bike up to him, he kept working the hoe as if he didn't know I was on the planet.

"We had a deal."

He acted as if he didn't hear me.

"We had a deal that I would sell popcorn for you and you'd fix my bike chain. Well, I sold popcorn for you."

After what seemed like forever, he said, "I'll have to borrow your tools."

"That's fine."

He walked over to our shed and rummaged around until he found what he needed. He bent down and started to work on the chain. I was afraid it wouldn't take him long to get that link off, and I had to make good use of the time.

"I was wrong, Elliot."

He hesitated a split second, then kept on working.

"I made friends with you because I like you. I like Beth, too. But Willis isn't the same as you."

He shook his head to show he was disgusted with me.

"But it's true! He's nothing but nasty. His raccoon tackled me, which scared me to death. He pushed me down and made my knees bleed. He attacked me over a dumb nickel that I didn't even owe him! And that was all the first day I met him! Plus, he's lied *to* me and *about* me. I can't like him. I'm not sorry about that. But I was wrong to pretend to you that I thought he was an okay person. That's what I'm sorry for. I should have been truthful, but I was afraid you wouldn't be my friend."

My heart pounded like a sledgehammer against my ribs while Elliot worked on my bike. When he finished, he handed me the extra bike link, put the tools and hoe back into the shed, then closed it.

I hadn't moved. He came back to where I was standing. He finally looked at me and said, "So you can't see anything about Willis that's good. Is that right?"

A little hollyhock doll worked its way through my thoughts. But for all I knew, Beth could be allergic to hollyhocks and Willis had made them to be mean. Or maybe it hadn't been Willis who'd made them. She could have been confused about that. She was only four, after all. So I pushed the thought back down. "No," I said. "I can't see anything good about him."

Elliot ran his hand through his hair and looked off for a minute. Then he said, "Willis can't always help the way he acts. He's not all bad. He just needs special handling. I try to give him that. He could use more people in his life who try to give him that."

Then he went back over the fence that divided our yards. It might as well have been an ocean.

9

I spent most of my time indoors the next few days—which was a purely stupid thing to do, because when I was inside the house Nanna always put me to work. Still, what choice did I have? I'd apologized to Elliot and it hadn't done any good. Since I didn't know what to say to him now, I tried to avoid him. I also wanted to avoid Willis, just because he was Willis.

I couldn't avoid Beth, though. Nanna was fixing to visit her sister, Louise, in Michigan. Even though she'd be gone only one week, she didn't want Mrs. Merrill to forget how to drive a car. Every day the two of them went on a drive early in the morning, leaving me to babysit Beth. It wasn't really much work, though.

Nanna had me run all her errands in the afternoons. She always wrote her grocery list on the outside of an envelope and put money and coupons inside. I never even bothered looking at it before I left because her lists were so exact. If she wanted dishwashing detergent she'd write under the heading of Hanson's, "Thrill, large bottle, third aisle at rear." Sure enough, if you went down that third aisle at Hanson's A&P to the back of the store, you'd find Thrill.

I was just finishing up Wednesday's shopping when I looked at the last item. She'd made a new heading, Evan's, which meant Evan's Drugs. Then she'd written, "Toni Home Permanent. Ask what shelf it's on. Read box. See if rods included. If not, buy one bag permanent rods, medium size."

Mother and I both had a natural wave in our hair that never came out. Nanna's hair had been the same since I'd known her, coiled braids pinned on top of her head. I couldn't imagine what she wanted the Toni for.

When I got home, Nanna was sitting in a kitchen chair in the Merrills' yard. Her long white hair was wet and hanging straight down her back. Mrs. Merrill was combing it.

I carried the groceries to the back door, eyeing the two of them. They were talking low and laughing until Nanna saw me.

"Oh, Lydia! Did you get the Toni?"

"Yes, ma'am."

"Good, bring it out as soon as you put the groceries away, hear? I want to read the directions to Carolyn."

I couldn't walk away without saying something. "Nanna, what's going on? You can't mean to curl your hair with a permanent! They don't make rods big enough to wind your long hair on."

She seemed to be thinking it over. "You know, Lydia, you're absolutely right. My long hair won't go on those little bitty rods. So, Carolyn . . . I guess you'll just have to cut it off!"

She and Mrs. Merrill laughed as if it was the funniest thing they'd ever heard.

I put the groceries away, then handed Nanna the permanent and rods. She thanked me and went on chatting with Mrs. Merrill, who held Nanna's hair and ran her fingers through it. She chewed her bottom lip like someone having second thoughts.

Good, I thought. It's about time somebody came to her senses. But, no, she picked up the scissors and cut Nanna's hair straight across at the base of her neck. I felt as though she were cutting my skin when she did it. I looked at Nanna's face as the hair fell at her feet, but she was holding her glasses to her nose and reading the Toni instructions out loud.

Then Mrs. Merrill began cutting Nanna's hair shorter on top. Short as a man's! I couldn't stand to watch anymore. I got on my bike and left.

That night I came home to a new Nanna. I thought she looked as if she had white puffs of cotton stuck all over her head. But she giggled like a schoolgirl when Daddy asked if she was Mother's younger sister. Even Mother joined in and said she was getting jealous of Daddy flirting with Nanna.

Nanna kept saying, "Oh, you two! Won't Louise be surprised when she sees me?"

"She'll think you're a movie star," Daddy said.

Nanna laughed at that. "I told Carolyn she has a real knack for hair. I told her I'd never have let just anybody cut my hair.

Why, I had twenty years of growth hanging down my back to prove that! But it was plain as day that she could do hair. Don't you love hers? I keep telling her, she's the spitting image of Jackie Kennedy."

When I went upstairs to bed, I stopped at Nanna's room to say goodnight. From the doorway I saw her reach up as if to touch her hair, then stop halfway and drop her hand. It landed palm up on her dresser, overturning a bowl of bobby pins, which spilled out onto the vanity.

I watched her face in the mirror. She didn't even blink at the noise the bowl made. Despite the way she acted about her new hairdo, she had the same sad look on her face that she got when she heard some elderly person from our church had died.

The change in Nanna was nothing compared to the one I saw in Mrs. Merrill. She had stopped wearing that worn-out green suit. Instead she wore what looked like boy's clothes. I figured she took Willis's and Elliot's too-small shirts and pants for herself.

It might sound funny, but she looked better in them than she ever did in her fancy old suit. They were threadbare but clean. She rolled the pants up and they looked like pedal pushers. She wasn't afraid to borrow our clothesline now, and one day I saw her with a pan of water scrubbing the windows of her house with a newspaper. It was as if she woke up and realized she had things to take care of.

And Beth! She seemed to be getting the most out of the change in Mrs. Merrill. Her face was always scrubbed now, and her stringy hair was in either a ponytail or pigtails tied with old pieces of ribbon. She looked right pretty.

I made it a point to whistle when I first saw Beth in her new hairdo. "Woo, Beth! You look mighty fine today!"

"Mamma fixed my hair! She says when I'm older, she'll give me a Toni Home Permanent!"

Oh Lord.

Friday night, Nanna was the first one ready for the Free Show. She took Daddy's arm and walked with her head held high.

Nanna settled herself on the benches Daddy and Sam had finally put in. Mrs. Beulah Duvall spotted Nanna as soon as we got there. Her mouth dropped open and she said, "Good heavens, Lydia Baldwin! What did you go and do to yourself?"

"I believe I improved myself, Beulah. I found the most wonderful beautician, right here in Maywood. She gave me a modern hairdo. Why, no one wears coiled braids anymore."

Mrs. Duvall wore a crown of braids. I held my breath. Nanna stared at her. Mrs. Duvall mumbled that she had something to see to. When she scurried away, Nanna took one last shot at her. "Beulah! If you'd like the name of that beautician, you just let me know. You hear?"

I broke out laughing. Nanna winked at me. I sat next to her and threw my arms around her. I gave her the biggest hug I could.

"Why, baby! What's this for?"

"No reason, Nanna. I just love you. That's all."

Monday was another hot day. The temperature kept climbing, and the higher it climbed, the lonelier I felt, since Elliot still wasn't talking to me.

I'd finished my chores early that morning and watched Beth while Nanna and Mrs. Merrill drove to the license branch to get Mrs. Merrill's driver's license.

Nanna seemed even happier about it than Mrs. Merrill did. After Beth and Mrs. Merrill went home, Nanna said, "She passed those tests with flying colors."

Nanna took off her hat, put on her apron, and turned back into her old bossy self. "Why don't you find something to do outside," she said. "I'm so busy today I don't need a youngster underfoot."

Nanna's train was leaving in two days for Great-Aunt Louise's.

I went outside, but Willis was playing with Zorro in his backyard. I decided I'd rather get into trouble for being "underfoot" than have to talk to him. I wandered to my room, but it was too stuffy. When I no longer heard Nanna rattling dishes, I grabbed Robert's picture out of its hiding place, then headed to the kitchen.

I stared at Robert, thinking that if I looked at him hard enough, he would give me the solution to my problem with Elliot. It didn't work.

I walked into the kitchen and set the photo down while I poured a glass of ice tea. Voices were coming from the living room. Nanna had *As the World Turns* on the television set. She always set up the ironing board in front of the TV to watch her soap operas, which were the dumbest shows I'd ever seen.

I made my way into the living room, where Nanna was holding a bottle of water with a sprinkler attached to the top. She sprinkled the clothes until they were damp, then rolled them up. She ironed them one by one, while some lady named Lisa griped about her husband, Bob, on television.

Normally I avoided ironing time because of the soap operas, but since Nanna was going to Louise's on Wednesday, I wanted to stay near her. I knew she never meant it when she threatened not to return. Still, that always made me a little nervous.

"Hi, Nanna." I flopped down on the sofa.

"Feet on the floor, young lady. What brings you in here? I know how you hate my soaps." She looked over the top of her glasses. "I also know you didn't show up to help with the ironing."

"No, ma'am. I'm just feeling kind of restless."

"Restless? Need me to give you a job?"

"Nah, it's not that." I set my ice tea on a coaster. "Nanna? Can you tell me another Robert story?"

"Another Robert story? Well, let me think of one I haven't told you."

"Yes, Nanna, let's hear *another* Robert story."

I sprang upright on the sofa. Mother stood in the kitchen door, holding the picture of Robert I had left by the refrigerator.

"Mother." The word came out as a plea. I wasn't sure for what.

"Maybe you could start by explaining why Robert's father isn't in this picture," Mother said. "I'm sure you're the one who tore it in half, right, Nanna? Lydia wouldn't have any reason to tear Philip out of the photo, but you do." When no one said anything, Mother asked a little louder, "I said, isn't that right, Nanna?" She spit out the question one word at a time.

Nanna took a newly ironed blouse and hung it on a hanger, as if nothing serious were going on. "Why are you home so early, Evelyn?"

"I have a headache. Now answer my question."

"Yes, I did tear it in half. Philip was Robert's daddy and he's not related to Lydia. He has nothing to do with her."

"Or me, anymore! Or you! Isn't that what you want to say? Oh, I can just hear your thoughts: 'He's dead now, thank God! No more Philip around. Let's get rid of any evidence that he ever lived.' I know how your mind works." Mother's voice kept getting higher. "And why does Lydia know about Robert? There was no reason for her to know. All these years I thought she didn't. Why did you go behind my back and tell her?"

I was on my feet, ready to say that Nanna hadn't told me. It was Daddy, and only because I'd overheard a private conversation. It was all my fault. But they didn't give me a chance.

"You were Robert's mother, but that doesn't mean you own him," Nanna said. "He's Lydia's brother. She has a right to know about him." She was so very calm.

"Oh, I get it. You've been filling her mind with stories that she's not an only child, is that it? Like she's got this—" She smacked the picture with the back of her hand for emphasis. Then her face crumpled and her voice softened as she said, "This fourteen-year-old brother." She looked up and her voice gained strength. "Well, did it occur to either of you that Robert would be close to thirty years old now? That even if he were here, he wouldn't be, oh, I don't know, riding bikes and walking her to school? What thirty-year-old wants a little girl hanging around?"

She was right. I guess I'd pictured him being fourteen forever.

"That's enough!" Nanna scolded. "Evelyn, you're getting hysterical."

"Hysterical? Maybe so. Maybe I was *hysterical* when I let Glen ask you to come live with us. Maybe I was *hysterical* for ever thinking I could stand having you in my life day after day."

In a quiet voice Nanna said, "But who would have raised the baby, Evelyn? You could barely stand to hold her."

I felt a sob start in my chest and explode from my lips. Nanna and Mother looked at me. Before they could say anything more, I ran out of the room.

Deep down I knew Mother didn't want me. I'd always known it. Hearing the words out loud, though, made me feel that I'd just been murdered but my body didn't have the good sense to die.

10

I left the house through the back door. Zorro must have climbed over the fence into our yard because I tripped over him. I heard Willis yelling at me, but my head didn't let his words come through.

I scrambled to my feet and took off without a thought to

where I was going. I just kept running. I don't know how long I ran. I know there came a time when I couldn't run anymore, so I walked. It was a blistering hot afternoon, the kind on which you could see squiggles rise up off the road. I ran again, until I heard a strange buzzing in my ears. Suddenly it seemed as if night was closing in on the outside of my vision. Then my legs felt like rubber and I slid to the ground.

Once I hit, my head started to clear. Lying there, I realized I must have fainted. I tried to figure out where I was. I slowly sat up and looked around. I was almost at the old Pearson place. I crawled until I was in the shade of a tree along the road. I knew that at the Pearsons' there was a hand pump in the yard and a porch where I could rest, so I figured I'd better keep going. I knew I'd never make it back home in that heat without water.

I wasn't sure I *could* go back home. No wonder Mother didn't want me. I made the biggest messes out of everything. I'd promised Daddy I wouldn't let Mother know that I knew about Robert. He'd warned me she wasn't strong enough to talk about him. Daddy probably wouldn't want me anymore, either.

After a time, I made myself get up. Didn't any cars ever drive down this road? I thought of poor old Mrs. Pearson and how lonely she must have been way out here. I bet it had been call for excitement to see the dust of a car driving by.

When I got to the Pearson place, I'd have cried for joy if I'd had any energy left in my body. I went to the hand pump. It squeaked from lack of use. I was worried that the well had gone dry, but finally, out came golden, rusty water. I let it run to get the rust out but also to bring up the cold water from deep in the ground. I cupped my hands and drank and drank. Then I sat under the pump and let that cold water pour right on top of my head. At first it was almost painful to my hot body. After the shock, though, it felt so good!

I made my way to the porch. What a shame there was no porch swing anymore. It would have made a fine place to rest. I sat down, leaned my back against the house, and stretched my tired feet in front of me. I closed my eyes for a minute, too exhausted to even think about Mother and the damage I'd done.

I heard a noise and raised my head. I must have fallen asleep because it was dark and I was curled up on the porch. I could hear crickets, but it was another noise that had awakened me.

"Lydia!"

"Daddy? Daddy! I'm here. I'm on the porch!"

He was there in two seconds.

"Are you all right, baby?"

"Sure. Well, tired. Tired and sore, I guess."

"I've been looking for you for hours, Ladybug." He grabbed me in a bear hug. He said, in a voice that didn't sound like his usual one, "I finally found someone who saw you head this way, but I never dreamed you'd really come this far."

Then I remembered everything.

"Oh, Daddy. I'm so sorry. I left Robert's picture out and Mother found it."

"Hush."

"No, Daddy, you've got to know. Mother's having a fit. I've

never seen her like that. And you told me not to let this happen. I'm so sorry, Daddy." I buried my wet face in his chest.

"I know. I know all about that. Nobody's mad at you. Come on, let's get you back home." He led me to the car, easing me into the seat as if I might break.

We drove for a few minutes without saying anything. He must really be mad at me. It wasn't like Daddy to let silence happen. He always needed to fill it up.

"Daddy—"

He interrupted me. "Honey, there's something I gotta say."

Here it comes, I thought. Now that he's over finding me, he's going to yell at me. Well, I deserve it.

"Nanna feels it might be best if she extends her visit in Michigan."

"For how long?"

"Well, she didn't say. Long enough to give her and your mother time to cool off, I guess."

"No!" I yelled, afraid Nanna would stay away forever.

"Now, Ladybug."

"It's not fair to make her leave! This was my fault. Nanna can't go, Daddy! She's part of us!"

"Now, first off, no one's telling Nanna to leave. She done this all on her own. And second, it's not about you, Lydia. It's about Nanna and Mother and how they don't get along too good."

"But Nanna wouldn't have thought about leaving us if Mother hadn't told her she'd made a mistake letting her come live with us. Don't you see, Daddy?"

He winced at that. "Well, things get said in anger that would be better left unsaid. Still and all, Mother didn't ask her to leave. You know how much Nanna looks forward to visiting Louise. It was her idea to stay longer."

"I don't believe you."

"Now, Lydia, I want you to be grownup about this. I know it pains you. I don't want her to go, either. And you're right. She *is* part of our family. But you know as well as I do that she and your mother are like oil and water. It might do us all good if we had a little break, don't you think?"

Even though he reached across the seat and held my hand, I felt as if I didn't know Daddy at that moment. I had the strangest feeling that someone else had picked me up and was pretending to be my daddy. I wondered if I was still dreaming on the porch. I'd spent my whole life listening to him keeping the peace between Mother and Nanna, and now he was just letting Nanna leave.

I shouldn't have run away. I should have stayed and made Mother see this was my fault, not Nanna's.

"Daddy?"

"Hush, now." He squeezed my hand. "It's settled."

Or maybe I should have kept running.

When I got home, Nanna was waiting on the front porch. She came down the porch steps sideways, holding on to the banister as though she didn't trust herself to get down them the way she did every other day. Daddy parked in front, and Nanna held her arms out. I ran into them crying.

"Oh, Lydia! Oh, baby."

"Nanna, I'm sorry."

"Now, you listen to me. You've got nothing to be sorry about."

I had that strange feeling again, like this wasn't Nanna, either. Nanna would have chewed my ear off for running away and worrying everyone.

She led me into the house, where Mother was on the phone.

"Oh, Glen's found her! I guess it was a false alarm, after all. So sorry to have bothered you, Clancy."

When I heard Mother say that into the phone—as if I'd caused her a little worry by not being home for supper, but now she could go on about her business—then I knew I wasn't dreaming. Mother was acting the way she always did.

Daddy reached out and ran his hand over my hair. I jerked away and passed Mother without a word. I went upstairs to the bathroom. I filled the bathtub to the top and soaked in it for a long time. I didn't want to get out. I was afraid of what was waiting for me on the other side of the door.

When I walked into my room, Nanna was sitting on my bed. She'd brought up a tray of milk and cookies. I wondered who would bring me milk and cookies if she left and burst into tears all over again.

"Come here, baby."

She tucked me into bed and handed me the tray. I drank a little milk but just pushed the cookies around.

She set the tray on my nightstand, then lay down with me in my bed. "Lydia, I know your Daddy told you about my plans. I want you to know that this isn't because of the words your mother and I had today."

I snorted.

"Well, it's not *just* about them. How's that? I've been giving some thought to staying with Louise for more than just one week a year, anyway. I lived with her once before, you know, when your mother married Robert's daddy. Married Philip." She made a point of saying his name.

"What is it about Philip, Nanna? Mother thinks you didn't like him."

"Oh, now, I never said I didn't like him. It's just that he drank. He drank a lot. I guess you could say he was an alcoholic. But he was such a fun-loving man that Evelyn couldn't see past that. Fun or no, I didn't think he was good husband material, and I said so. I sometimes think that made Evelyn marry him even faster, knowing I didn't approve. So Evelyn and Philip moved from Michigan to Ohio, and I moved in with my sister."

"Louise had a husband, and her grandchildren always dropped by to visit. I didn't feel useful to her then, but now she's all alone. I've been thinking she and I might be good companions for each other. We're too old to do all that bickering that sisters do." She smiled at me.

I didn't smile back. "Why does it have to be this week? Can't you trade your train ticket in for one next week?"

"I was all set to go now, anyway. All I have to do is throw in a few more clothes than I'd planned on."

"But what about me, Nanna?"

Her eyes got watery. She cleared her throat and said, "You? Why, you'll be just fine. I'm expecting you to keep things up around here until I get back."

"When will that be?"

"I can't give you a date, Lydia. We're just going to see how things go."

"Will you be back before school starts?"

"Probably not."

"*When*, then?"

"I promise I'll see you at Thanksgiving if not before."

"You'll move back by Thanksgiving?"

"Or visit . . . depending on how things go."

I started to argue, but she said, "We're not discussing this anymore. I have clothes to pack and you need your sleep. You look worse than a stray cat."

Then Nanna did something she hadn't done for years. She turned out the light and ran her fingers through my hair while singing the songs she put me to sleep with every night when I was little.

I couldn't sleep, but I pretended to, and Nanna eventually left my room. Daddy must have been waiting for her in the hall. I sat up and strained to hear their conversation.

"She'll be fine. She's just tired," Nanna said.

"I think I'll go in and make sure she's all right. She's awful upset about you leaving."

"She's asleep. Let her be, Glen."

"Well . . ." Daddy hesitated for a minute, then said, "Do you realize how far she walked today? I'm thankful I looked there."

Their voices lowered and I couldn't make out the words until Daddy said, "It won't even give you time to pack properly. Why don't you wait and catch the train next week?"

"Oh, Glen, it would only make it harder on me. I'd spend all my time cooking casseroles and worrying everybody to death about how to do the things I do every day. It's exactly the kind of thing that would drive Evelyn up the wall. It will be easier on all of us if I go on Wednesday."

More murmuring, then Nanna said, "I told Lydia I'd come for Thanksgiving."

They walked down the hall and their voices were lost to me.

What seemed like hours later, I heard Zorro's clattering. Then I heard something else. I got up to look out the window.

On the roof of the Merrills' place I saw the silhouette of a person. I jumped back from the window. Slowly I peeked around the curtain and realized that it was Willis. He wasn't moving. He wasn't looking into our windows or anyone else's. He just sat there staring up at the sky as if deep in thought.

11

I held the phone tight to my ear and waited for Rae Anne's mom to get her. Rae Anne was my best friend, but I had had to ask the operator for her number. I'd always been so used to having her next door or seeing her at school that it never occurred to me before that I could call her on the telephone.

"Lydia? Is something wrong?"

"No, nothing's wrong. Haven't you ever gotten a telephone call before?"

"Well, yeah. Sure I have. But never from you."

"I just wondered if you could talk your folks into coming to the Free Show this week, that's all." News traveled fast in

Maywood and I didn't want to face all the questions about Nanna's leaving on my own.

"Oh, I can tell you the answer to that. No. But I wouldn't want to, anyway. Darryl is coming home on leave!"

It had been almost a year since Darryl had been home from the army. "Ask Darryl to drive you. I'd like to see him, too."

"I wish I could. He's bringing a special girl. They're here for the weekend, then he's going to meet her parents. I think they're in *love*."

"Well, that's great. I guess."

"Lydia Carson, what's wrong?"

Boy, where would I start on that question?

"Nothing, really. Nanna's gone. She left yesterday. She's visiting her sister in Michigan, at least until Thanksgiving."

"Bet you're doing cartwheels over that!"

"Cartwheels?"

"All I ever hear is you complaining about the stuff Nanna makes you do or the stuff Nanna won't let you do. Congratulations! You've got the whole summer to yourself!"

"Yeah, um, thanks."

"I'll talk to my parents, though. Maybe I can visit in a few weeks. I'll see if I can spend the night. With Nanna gone, we'll stay up till midnight and eat in bed!"

"Oh, Rae Anne!" I gripped the phone with both hands, as if that would bring her closer to me. "That would be swell!"

I hung up feeling a little better. Nanna had only been gone a day, but since she left the house seemed to have grown. Sometimes I'd walk in and the hallway would look so long! And the silence was louder than any noise I ever heard.

I wandered to the porch and saw Mrs. Merrill bring her

kitchen chair into her yard, the way she did when she fixed Nanna's hair. I would have spoken to her, but she led Willis out of the house and started cutting his hair real short. Funny how he let her do that. I'd have thought he'd put up a fight.

When Daddy and Mother came home that night, Mother was talking to Daddy a mile a minute. She was so happy it hurt me to look at her. How could she be happy with Nanna taking off like that?

"Oh, Lydia! I was just telling your dad about our new schedule. Come sit down and I'll go over it with both of you."

She pulled her notebook out of her skirt pocket and sat down. She smiled brightly at us.

"I was saying we need some sort of schedule to divide up the work Nanna did. I'll do the cooking, and your father will wash the dishes."

"Sounds fair to me," Daddy said.

"Lydia, will you pick up the mail?" she said.

I nodded.

"We'll make our own beds each day and we'll all three do the heavy cleaning on Sunday mornings."

Daddy fidgeted in his chair a little. "Well, after Lydia and I get back from church, you mean."

"Oh, church, right." Mother looked back at her list, frowned, and wrote something down. "Well, we'll do it after. That leaves laundry. I'll do the ironing whenever I can. Now, Lydia, since your father and I both work during the day, I thought you could wash the clothes. I know Nanna had you hanging them out and taking them down anyway. You might as well do the washing."

"On the wringer washer?" I asked. Besides being an awful

lot of work, the wringer was dangerous—I saw Nanna almost run her fingers through it once. She had me quickly unplug it, and she was all right, but that had scared the daylights out of me.

"Oh, that contrary old beast. Glen, why don't you call Sam Green and get a new automatic washing machine?"

"No!" I yelled. As much as I hated the wringer, Nanna always said she wouldn't be caught dead using anything else. "Nanna would hate a new automatic. We have to keep it."

Daddy smiled an indulgent smile and said, "Now, Lydia, I know Nanna loves that old machine, but she won't stay away if we buy a new one." He chuckled.

Well, none of this was funny to me. "I'll keep the wringer."

"Of all the silly things. Let her, Glen. She'll be begging for a new one after she has a week or so of that old washer."

When Mother said that, something changed in me. I looked at her smiling that cat-that-got-the-cream smile and wondered why I ever cared whether she loved me or not.

I held up Daddy's T-shirt—whites. My jeans—colors. Daddy's red bandanna. Nanna always said that reds had to be washed with other reds and that was that. I set it aside for when I had a full load of red stuff. Sorting the clothes was easy compared to washing them.

I did all right at first. I'd seen Nanna fill the washer enough times. She never changed the water. She went from washing whites to light colors to darks all in the same water. I put the washing powder in it and then the white clothes. After they agitated for a bit, I stopped the machine and fed the clothes through the wringer. Then I plopped them into a tub of clean water to rinse.

Everything went fine until I put Daddy's good white shirt in the wringer. I heard a crunch, and then—*ping!*—a button went flying across the room. I hurried and unplugged the wringer. Every single one of the buttons was crushed except for the one that flew off.

I kicked that old wringer washer. Dang, dang, dang! Then I kicked it again. I'd never hear the end of it if Mother saw that shirt. I didn't know how to sew on buttons and didn't even know where Nanna kept her button jar. Finally I wadded the shirt up and threw it in the trash can. I put a newspaper on it and dumped wet coffee grounds on top for good measure. No one would go digging under those. Daddy might wonder where his shirt was, but then he was always forgetting things.

I was plumb exhausted by the time I carried that first load upstairs, and I still had two more loads to do. I opened the door to the back porch to get Nanna's clothespin apron and ran smack into Mrs. Merrill.

"Oh, Lydia!" She grabbed her chest. "You scared me to death."

"I'm sorry, Mrs. Merrill. I didn't know you were here."

"Well, it's Friday. It's the day Nanna lets me borrow your clothesline. I was just coming for the clothespins."

She reached for the apron and said, "I can't wait until Nanna comes back next week. A lady, Mrs. Duvall, came by and asked if I would perm her hair just like Nanna's. Can you believe it?"

Then it hit me like a ton of bricks. Mrs. Merrill didn't know that Nanna wasn't coming back. I suppose Nanna had been so frazzled about leaving that she hadn't thought to tell her.

"Lydia, is something wrong?"

"Well, Mrs. Merrill, I guess . . . yes. Yes, ma'am. There's something you don't know." I felt my tongue getting heavy. I couldn't quite make the words come out.

"What is it?"

I took a deep, ragged breath. "Nanna isn't here. She's visiting her sister in Michigan. She's gonna be there a while."

"I do know that. She told me she visits her for a week every year."

"I know, ma'am, but she decided to go for a longer time. I don't know when she'll be back. It was a last-minute decision, or I'm sure she'd have told you."

A tiny "Oh" came out of Mrs. Merrill. If I hadn't seen her mouth form a small circle, I wouldn't have known she'd said it. She looked as if her bones went limber, as if she'd shrunk. It made me want to say something nice to her.

"Mrs. Merrill?"

"Yes?" She looked up.

"Well, ma'am." My brain froze. I couldn't think of anything nice about Nanna's leaving. "I was just going to say that I'll be doing the laundry now, and I'm not particular about what day I do it like Nanna was. So you can use the clothesline any day you want."

"Oh. Okay. Well . . . thank you, Lydia."

For the first time, I realized that Nanna was probably the only person Mrs. Merrill really knew in town.

"Um, Mrs. Merrill, I don't suppose you know how to use a wringer washer, do you?"

"My mother had one for years." She smiled, remembering.

"Is there some special trick to not ruining buttons?"

"Buttons and zippers. Yes, there is."

"Ma'am, do you think you could come inside for just a minute to show me?"

With Mrs. Merrill's help, I learned how to work the wringer. By the time the clothes had dried on the line and I'd folded them and put them away, Mother and Daddy were home from work.

You'd have thought Mother was a teenager, she was so excited about going to the show with Daddy. It was hard even to look at her.

"You ready, Ladybug?" Daddy called from the door.

"I'm not goin' tonight," I said. "There's a movie on television I'd rather see."

Truth was, I didn't know what was on. I didn't want to go with them.

"But you love the Free Show." Daddy's eyes showed concern.

"If she'd rather stay home, it's fine, Glen," Mother said. "Don't push her."

"Well, if you're sure . . ." he said as he followed Mother out the door.

I flipped on the TV, thinking there was surely something on as good as the movie showing tonight, *The Fastest Gun Alive*. I tried but I couldn't really concentrate on anything, because I suddenly remembered the serial. How could I miss seeing what happened next with Buck Rogers?

I waited until it was almost dark and headed for the Free Show alone.

"I didn't have time to make a pie, mind you, but we *are* having dessert!" Mother twittered Monday night as she went into the kitchen. I hated how happy she was these days.

"If it tastes like dinner did, I don't want any," I told Daddy.

"Ladybug! Shame on you. Your mother worked all day and still put out this fine spread."

"Fine spread of what? Did you know what we were eating? I sure didn't."

"Well, she'll learn," Daddy said as he eyed his plate. I could tell he wasn't sure, either.

We heard a dish crash to the floor and Mother scream, *"Gleennnn!"*

We raced into the kitchen. Mother was backed into a corner, holding a chair in front of her like a lion tamer. She saw us and pointed to the screen door. Zorro was hanging on to the outside with his arms and legs spread wide.

I let out a hoot of laughter.

"I'm glad you're getting such a kick out of this, young lady," Mother said indignantly. "That mangy thing nearly scared me to death."

"He must have smelled your cooking," Daddy said as he poked at the screen, trying to get Zorro down.

I'd gotten into the habit of feeding Zorro peanut butter but had forgotten about it since Nanna left. He must have missed it a lot. Maybe I'd sneak out and give him an extra helping tonight as thanks, seeing as how he made Mother forget all about giving us dessert—one less dish of hers I had to eat.

The phone rang, and Mother set the kitchen chair back down and reached for it. "Hello? Why, hello, Clancy. How are you this evening? Glen? Yes, he's here. Just a minute, please."

She handed the telephone to Daddy.

Sheriff Yates sometimes called to tell Mother some bit of news he wanted in the paper. That always gave me a little thrill, since it meant I knew the goings on in town before anyone else, so I stayed in the kitchen.

"Clancy! How's the peacekeeping business? You don't say! No, I didn't realize they don't have a phone. Well, sure. It'll be a mite awkward, but I'd hate for her to worry about him all night. I'll tell her. Thanks, Clancy."

Daddy hung up the phone and looked from me to Mother. "Little pitchers have big ears," he said, meaning he didn't want me to hear. He still thought I didn't know what that meant. Daddy used to spell words in front of me, too, long after I knew how to read.

I said, "I'll clear the table," and walked into the dining room. Of course, all I did was get on the other side of the kitchen door and listen.

"I guess Boyd Merrill and some boys got a little drunk after work tonight. He was arrested for disturbing the peace. Clancy said the Merrills don't have a phone and asked me to tell his wife."

Mr. Merrill arrested! Nanna was right. He *was* a drunk.

Daddy asked Mother, "Would you like to come with me?"

"No!" Mother said real fast. Then she said, "It's bad enough you know about it. Can you imagine how embarrassed she's going to feel?"

I heard Daddy stirring around, so I quickly stacked some dishes and carried them into the kitchen. Daddy said in a too loud voice, "Ladies, I'll be back quick as a wink. Got a little something to take care of."

"I'm getting a headache," Mother said. "I think I'm going to lie down."

It seemed to me that Mother was taking this whole thing bad for someone who didn't know the Merrills all that well. Maybe Mr. Merrill's drinking reminded her of her husband Philip's.

"I'll get the dishes when I come back, Evelyn. You run on to bed." Daddy got his hat and walked out the front door.

I carried more dishes into the kitchen until I heard Mother's feet on the stairs. Then I sneaked out the front door and crept slowly toward the Merrills' house. I wanted to hear Daddy and Mrs. Merrill, but all I heard was that infernal Zorro.

There I was, crouched down with Zorro on the loose. Naturally, Zorro took that as an invite to climb up my back. I gave myself credit for not screaming or hurling him off this time. Instead I staggered around to the back of the house while he hung on.

"Hey, Zorro!" Willis threw open the back screen door and smirked. "What kind of trash did you drag home?"

"Oh, very funny!" I said. "Get him off me, will ya?"

He grabbed Zorro with one hand and shoved me with the other. I landed on my knees.

"Would you stop that, Ratboy!"

"*Ratboy?* Why are you callin' me that?" He didn't look so happy now. "And what were you doin'? Tryin' to steal my raccoon?"

This was the Willis I knew. I couldn't convince him of anything. But because of Elliot, I tried.

"Willis. Listen to me. I promise I'm telling the truth.

You'd better not let Zorro run loose. He scared my mother tonight by hanging on our screen door. If he does that to the wrong person, he could get hurt."

"You liar. That's all you do is lie. I don't let Zorro run loose, and he can't get out of that cage by himself, now, can he?"

"Well, yeah, he probably can. He's pretty smart. Maybe you should put a cement block or something heavy like that in front of his door."

"That tears it. That just tears it. Leave us alone. And don't you be telling me what to do with my coon, y'hear?"

He stomped away with Zorro, and I saw Daddy doing the dishes in our kitchen window. Shoot! I'd missed it all on account of that knot-head, Willis Merrill.

12

I didn't mind making my own bed with Nanna gone. Nobody cared how wrinkled it looked. So far that was about the only good thing about her being gone.

The days sure were long. I'd have given anything to be able to run over and see Mrs. Ogle, whether Rae Anne was there or not. I also missed Elliot something awful. He spent most of his time working at the Oasis. When I saw him in our garden, I always found some excuse to run outside to be near him. He would nod, but that was all.

I was getting pretty good at the laundry, but I hated doing it. Dirty clothes were stacking up. Then on Thursday morning Mother said, "Now, Lydia, don't forget to put clean sheets on the beds."

I went to the basement with enough sheets to make up two loads, right there. I felt as if I lived in the basement on wash days. I decided to come up with a plan.

I stuffed the sheets into a dark corner of the basement. We had lots of sheets. No reason those had to be washed right away. Then I went through all the clothes that were mine and checked to see if there were any spills on them. The ones that passed that test got the sniffing test. If they weren't too smelly, I took them up to my room and hung them back on hangers. That cut out a load, at least.

Daddy's clothes all had to be washed, since he worked up a sweat at his job. There was grease on just about everything he owned. Then I moved on to Mother's. She wore a skirt and blouse to work each day, but she wore a printer's apron over them. Some of the blouses had smudges on the sleeves, so I washed those. The skirts didn't look dirty. I gave them the sniff test. Mother's work clothes always smelled like graphite and oil. I carried her skirts outside to air them out on the line. There! All I needed was a system.

I went into the house to get some ice tea. Unfortunately, none of us had remembered to fill the ice cube trays. It made me miss Nanna. I'd been thinking about writing her. I should write and tell her about how much better Mrs. Merrill was doing. Nanna would be so proud of her. She was using our clothesline, and even the day after Mr. Merrill was arrested, she came out and swept off her porch as if nothing had happened.

I wished then and there that I could be more like Nanna. If I were, I probably could give Willis "special handling," the way Elliot did. Then Elliot and I could be friends again. But I wasn't like Nanna, and I thought Willis might have been too much even for her.

June 21, 1962

Dear Nanna,
    Bet you never thought you'd get a letter from me.

I chewed on the pencil and rolled over on my bed. This was harder than I thought. If I told her about Mother's cooking it might make her worry that we'd all starve. I decided to keep things light in my first letter.

    Nothing much has changed around here. Mrs. Merrill sure misses you but she's doing real fine. Why, you'd never have known that Mr. Merrill was in jail if Sheriff Yates hadn't called us. And she's doing something to every head she can get her hands on. Beth's hair is always fixed up real nice. She cut Willis's hair short. I think they call it a crew cut. I hope his pet raccoon doesn't get too close to her. He may end up looking like a poodle. Ha ha.
    I've been doing the laundry but don't worry. I haven't turned everything pink yet. Just kidding. Tell Great-Aunt Louise hello from her Great-Niece Lydia. I miss you, Nanna.

Love,
Lydia

P.S. Could you send us your recipe for buttermilk cookies?
Or if you have any extras made up, you could mail them
just like they do to soldiers on the front. Ha ha.

I reached for the envelope I'd brought with me. It must have fallen to the floor. I lowered my arm over the side of the bed, feeling around, when my hand landed on a book. I pulled it out. It was the library book I'd checked out about raccoons! I'd clean forgot it. My heart pounded as I looked at the stamped date. It was fifteen days overdue.

I pedaled to the library so hard I practically flew. Grabbing the book out of the basket on my bike, I ran up the steps and opened the heavy door. I paused inside and tried to catch my breath. Looking down at the floor inside the cool vestibule, I made myself count the tiny floor tiles. After I got to thirty, I was calm enough to walk in slowly.

"Good morning, Lydia!"

I jumped. Would I ever get used to loud Mrs. Green?

"Hello, Miz Green. I've got something just awful to tell you."

"Just awful? Oh, do tell." She put her elbows on her desk and rested her chin on her hands. I could see the corners of her mouth twitching.

"Well, ma'am, I forgot to bring this book back. I'm so sorry! I promise it will never happen again!" My words got faster, spilling one on top of the other. "I'll pay the late fee but, please, Miz Green—Nanna would have my hide if she knew!"

"Oh, honey. I surely do miss your Nanna, but how am I going to tell her about it with her up in Michigan? And you know what I always say? I always say, how can a book get read if it's sitting here on our shelves? Why, it doesn't bother me a bit when a book's late."

She leaned down and said in a whisper, "You might want to renew it next time, though. That way you won't have to pay late fees."

"Yes, ma'am," I said, wondering how much money this was going to cost me. A dollar a day, probably.

"That'll be thirty cents. Two cents a day. It's fifteen days overdue. I'm sorry to have to charge you, honey, but it's the rules."

"Oh, yes ma'am! That's just fine!" I was so relieved I almost slid to the floor as I counted out the change.

Mrs. Green picked up the book and said, "I remember this book. It was to impress that special fella of yours." She winked at me. "Did it work?"

"Miz Green, he's not my special anything." I thought of how my experiment with Zorro had ended, with Willis throwing Beth's doll into the burn barrel. "And, no, I guess you could say it was a complete disaster."

"Really? Well, maybe you just didn't use it right. Did you impress him with all you learned about raccoons?"

I let out a huff of air. "I can't say he was all that impressed."

"Maybe you should renew the book and try a new tack."

I started to say I didn't care one whit if Willis Merrill was impressed or not, but I caught myself. She had said, "Try a new tack." It made me think of what Elliot had said, that Willis needed "special handling."

"You know what, Miz Green? I think I might just renew that book, after all. That is, if it's all right with you."

"Why sure, honey! Never let it be said that Beverly Green stood in the way of true love!"

Good gosh.

Monday morning, I waited in the tree house for Willis. I wanted to catch him before he got to Zorro's cage. I knew Zorro would run to me and I'd lose any chance of having Willis listen.

As soon as he walked out the back door, I said, "He likes peanut butter."

Willis jumped at the sound of my voice. Normally it would have made me laugh, but I was trying a new tack today.

"You talkin' to me?"

"I said that Zorro likes peanut butter. Not as much as he likes nuts and fruit, but that's why he comes up here with me. I lured him with peanut butter."

"You think you know more about my coon than me?" He snickered and shook his head.

"It's all in here." I held up the library book. "It tells about raccoons and their likes and dislikes. For instance"—I thumbed quickly through the book—"it says right here, 'A raccoon is a nocturnal mammal.' That means they would rather sleep during the day and play at night."

Willis cocked his head and said, "Zorro sleeps at night."

"He's probably bored. That cage is none too big for him. If he were in the wild, he'd be running at night."

Willis seemed to be thinking about it for a minute. Then he waved one hand in the air as if to say I was as annoying as a fly. "You're crazy," he said. "You're making that up."

"No, I'm not. I know you don't like to read." He shot an angry look at me, so I hurried on. "I don't, either. Heck, this is the only book I've ever checked out of the library that I didn't have to. I wanted to trick you, so I read up on raccoons. That's the plain truth."

"Why are you telling me now?"

"I just didn't want you to think that Zorro liked me more than you, that's all."

"I *know* he doesn't like you more than me!"

Oh, he could make my blood boil! Well, I promised myself that I'd just make an attempt today. That's all I had to do and I'd done it.

I climbed out of the tree and made myself walk at a normal pace instead of storming into the house the way I wanted to. I had just reached the back door when Willis asked, "That book got any pictures in it?"

I read to him in the tree house for at least half an hour. Willis hung on to every word.

"I never knew there was so much to know about coons," he said.

"There's a lot in here about them," I said. "Where did you get Zorro anyway?"

"Found him in a ditch alongside a road. His mama had been hit by a car. He was a tiny thing, and look how big he is now." He pointed to Zorro's cage. "I did a good job raising him, even without that book!"

"Uh-huh," I said, hiding my irritation. I'd had enough of this. My voice was hoarse. I was thirsty. And I had to go to the bathroom, plain and simple. I finished reading the chapter, then said in my nicest voice, "Well, I guess that's about it for today. Maybe I could read more to you tomorrow."

"Tomorrow! You goin' somewhere or somethin'?"

"No, but we've read an awful lot. Aren't you getting thirsty?"

"No."

He picked up the book and shoved it at me. My hands caught it out of reflex, but I just sat there surprised. Then he pushed the book at me again and grunted for me to read more.

We must've looked like Tarzan and Jane, stuck in a tree house with him shoving and grunting. I laughed at the thought.

When Willis heard me laugh, he hauled off and slapped me right in the face.

I let out a yelp and grabbed my cheek. No one had ever slapped me before. And it hurt! My eyes were stinging something awful and I couldn't talk because I knew I'd sob if I did.

Willis did what he always did and scurried out of the tree house. I watched his lanky body trudge toward Zorro's cage. I hated him so much. If I had told anyone what had happened, that person would have said, "You did all you could, Lydia. That boy just can't be helped."

In the past, I would have yelled at him, but I knew Elliot wasn't going to like me again until I was nice to Willis. What if I changed how I acted? What if I didn't yell and get mad? Would Willis change, too? I took in great big gulps of air, trying to still the tears that threatened as I sat quietly watching him.

He got Zorro out of his cage, let the raccoon climb onto his back, and shot me a look. I was trying to keep my expression normal and made sure I looked right into his eyes. I'd read enough of this raccoon book to know that making eye contact was the best thing to do when dealing with a wild animal. How much wilder could you get than Willis Merrill?

He looked at me for a second, looked away, then looked back. He said, "You laughed at me."

I took another deep breath and said, "I was looking at you when I laughed. But I was laughing at what I was thinking about, not at you."

"Well, how's a body supposed to know the difference?" he said, heading back to the tree house.

"Wait! I'm coming down." I tried to keep my voice light. I didn't want to be cornered in the tree if he got violent again. I was willing to take this special handling thing only so far.

"Whew!" I said when I reached the ground. "It's sure getting hot. I'm really thirsty. Let's go inside and get something to drink."

Willis looked at my house and said, "I'll wait here."

"Suit yourself."

I turned to go and realized that's just the kind of thing I would have said before.

"How about this?" I asked. "How about I get us something to drink and we move to our front porch? It'll be cooler there, and I'll read some more."

He looked at the porch warily.

"I can make us Kool-Aid."

He brightened at that.

"Wait here. I'll be right back." I started inside, then turned to Willis. "Hold the book for me, okay?"

You'd have thought I asked him to watch a pot of gold from the look on his face.

"You got any more?" Willis asked as he handed me his empty glass. It was his second one.

"I'm only allowed two glasses of Kool-Aid a day. Besides, if we drink it all up today, we won't have any for tomorrow, right?"

He thought that over. "Okay."

This "special handling" of Willis was harder work than I'd guessed. I had to watch how I said everything. And I was trying real hard not to laugh. It made me tired. Plus I'd read more in one day than I normally read all summer.

I closed the book and asked, "Would you like to read more of the book tomorrow?"

"Yeah!"

"Okay. Can we make a deal?"

He jumped up and crossed his arms. "What's the hitch? I ain't got money if that's what you're after."

"Money! I don't want money. But you remember when you slapped me? It's not a nice thing to do to anybody."

"Neither's laughing."

"We talked about that, remember? I was laughing, but I wasn't making fun of you. There's a difference. How about we make some rules. Rule number one is no making fun of each other."

"What's rule number two?"

"Rule number two is that if we get mad, we say why we're mad. We never hit."

"Can we have Kool-Aid every day?"

I almost laughed but, thank goodness, caught myself. I very seriously said, "Rule number three, we have Kool-Aid every day."

"Three glasses of it."

"Don't push it, Willis."

13

I was feeling pretty good when I went in to dinner that night. Mother had a ham in the oven. How bad can you mess up a ham? Last night Mother had cooked a roast so dry you could hardly cut it. I'd filled up on mashed potatoes, eating around the lumps, and on the tops of dinner rolls—leaving the burnt bottoms.

I flopped into my chair. When Daddy asked, "How'd your day go, Ladybug?" I had something good to tell him for a change.

"Well, you know that boy from next door? Willis? I spent the afternoon reading to him."

"He can't read?"

Daddy looked confused, and I realized I hadn't told him about Willis Merrill. Something kept me from telling him how mean and ornery Willis could be. "No, not too good."

"So you're teaching him how?"

"Well, no, I guess I'll leave that to his teachers. But he loves to have a book read to him, so that's what I did."

Mother said, "Well, if he can get you to read, he's got my thanks."

What's it to you? I wanted to say to her. She had never before paid any attention to whether or not I read.

Then she set a plate of food in front of me. It was the same food as last night. I don't mean leftovers, I mean the very plate I had left unfinished the night before. The roast was drier now and the lumps of potatoes I'd picked out were still there, but cold, along with the burnt bottoms of the rolls.

"What's this?"

"It's your dinner. Eat up!" she said in a cheery voice.

"That's not funny. What is this, Daddy?"

He looked uncomfortable. "Um, I think I'll stay out of this one, ladies."

"Stay out of what?"

Mother sat down and flipped her napkin open before she laid it in her lap. "Well, Lydia, we all had jobs we agreed to do when Nanna left, isn't that correct? And yours was to wash the dirty clothes. Since you've chosen not to wash my clothes, and expect me to wear them dirty, I decided I'd return the favor. Why should I cook a new meal for you every day? I'll just let you eat what you left the night before." She smiled as she picked up her fork. "I guess your little plan saves us both some work, doesn't it?"

My face was hot with embarrassment. But more than that, I was angry.

"You know what? I'll save you even more work." I got up and threw my plate into the sink. "Don't bother cooking for me at all. The reason I had food left over is because I can't eat what you cook."

"Lydia!" Daddy said, but I wouldn't look at him.

"Fair enough," Mother said. "I've never claimed to be a gourmet."

"Gourmet? You can't boil water!" I shouted at her.

She went on as if I hadn't said a word. "But who gave you the right to decide which of my clothes should get washed, Lydia?"

"There's just so *much* laundry! You don't know how much work it is to wring all those clothes out and then rinse them and wring them out again."

Too late I remembered that Mother wanted to get rid of Nanna's washer.

"That's a problem you created for yourself, young lady. You can have a new washer any time you ask."

"You want to make it so Nanna never comes back. You might not care about her, but I miss her! If you think you can step in now and become my mother, you can forget it. I don't know why you didn't just ship me off with Nanna since you didn't want me to begin with."

Daddy stood up. In a stern voice I hardly recognized, he said, "Go to your room."

I looked at Daddy, who treated me so special until I was up against Mother. He took her side no matter what. And Mother—well, I didn't know what to make of her at all.

"That's a fine idea," I said. "There's nobody here I want to spend time with, anyway."

I flounced out of the kitchen, went to my bedroom, and gave my door the hardest slam I could muster. There's something satisfying about slamming a door when you're mad. It was something Nanna never understood. She'd have followed me upstairs, then made me come out into the hall and close the door quietly. Well, Nanna wasn't here.

The evening dragged on. I kept thinking that Daddy or Mother would eventually knock on my door with a plate of cookies or maybe a sandwich. Nanna would have. But I didn't hear a word from either of them. I was so hungry the front of my stomach felt as if it were touching my backbone. When I heard their footsteps coming to bed, I knew one of them would open the door to make sure I was all right. I was wrong again. After I heard their bedroom door close for the night, I finally gave in to the tears that had been threatening.

I was on the same bed, in the same house that I'd lived in my entire life, but nothing was familiar anymore. I didn't even have my picture of Robert since Mother had found it. I'd been losing people all summer, it seemed.

The next morning I waited until Mother and Daddy had left for work before getting up. I made a piece of toast and took it downstairs with me while I sorted the laundry—*all* the laundry. Then I washed the first load and carried it upstairs to hang outside.

Willis was sitting on the ground, leaning against the base of our oak tree. "You ready to read?"

"How long have you been there?" I asked in a not very friendly tone.

"You said we'd read every day."

I felt tired already and the day had just begun.

"Yeah, we will. It's just that I have to do my chores first. You know chores? Jobs? Don't you have any?"

"Nah."

"Well, I do. I have to hang up this laundry. Then I'll have to wash a second load. It's gonna take me a while."

"Get some help," he said, as if I were an idiot for not thinking of it.

"It's just me here."

"If I helped, you'd get done faster and we could read."

"Well . . . yeah . . . that would work." I wasn't sure I wanted to spend all day with Willis, but it would be nice to have help. "You sure you want to?"

He smiled and said, "Heck no, I don't want to. But I will."

I laughed at that, then quickly looked to see if he'd taken it wrong. He was smiling.

True to his word, Willis hung up the clothes while I wrung out the second load. The work went faster, and in no time we were ready to read. Then I went to the Frigidaire to get our Kool-Aid and saw a note stuck to the front:

Lydia,

    Please come by the newspaper shop when you get your work done.

Mother

She had never asked me to come there before. She always acted as if I were intruding if I so much as walked in. I wadded up the note, threw it into the trash, and carried the Kool-Aid out to Willis.

I wasn't going. She could come to me. Still, the whole time I was reading about the gestation period of raccoons, I wondered what Mother wanted. I was glad when our time was up and Willis left.

I ran into the bathroom and combed my hair. I looked in the mirror and said to my reflection, "You're pitiful." I hated myself for going.

I walked into the newspaper shop to a loud *ooga! ooga!* The horn sounded over the noise of the machinery to let Mother know when customers came in. I stood there, breathing in the sharp smell while I waited for her to look up from her Linotype machine.

It was a big machine that had a sort of typewriter attached, and the letters were all scrambled up but in a different order than on a typewriter. The machine had a small pot of melted metal, and when Mother hit enough keys to fill up a line of type she would send the line through the machine. The melted metal would be molded into a line of type. That's how it got its name, Linotype. Then she'd type the next line and it would follow.

I knew all that because our second-grade class had taken a field trip here. Mother had typed every student's name and they'd gotten to take the molded letters home. I still remember our teacher, Mrs. Howard, saying, "Lydia, we won't do yours. You probably have tons of these at home."

I'd just smiled a stupid smile while my heart sank. I would have given my eyeteeth to have one of those little metal names made by Mother. I wished I could go back to that moment and say, "No, Mrs. Howard. My mother never cared enough about me to let me come watch her work or type my name for me."

"Hello, Lydia." Mother brought me back to the present.

"Hi," I said.

She wiped her hands on a rag and said, "I'm so glad you came by. I was thinking about our conversation last night and, well"—she gave a little laugh—"cooking is proving more difficult than I thought."

I didn't say anything.

"But then you already know that," she said wryly. "Anyway, I may as well be honest here. I've never had to cook before. You see, Philip . . . my first husband . . . You, of course, know about him."

I stayed silent.

"Well, he was a fantastic cook. He owned a restaurant and brought dinner home every night. Wasn't I smart to marry someone like him?" She smiled, but the smile didn't reach her eyes. "When your father and I married, we ate at the Oasis most nights. Then Nanna came and took over. I actually looked forward to being the cook for the first time in my life, but everything takes so long! Why, half the time I forget to thaw the meat and by the time I get anything on the table it's late."

She pulled her chair around from the Linotype to face me and sat down. "So! I wondered if you had any suggestions."

"You mean you want me to cook?"

"Oh, no. You have enough to do."

Well, at least she noticed that!

"Lydia, would you be terribly disappointed if we had, say, lunch-meat sandwiches some nights? Oh, I know it's not what Nanna would fix but—"

"Nah, I wouldn't mind." Nanna never let me eat it, but I had baloney with cheese and ketchup with Rae Anne at Mrs. Ogle's house.

"Good! And I was thinking that maybe we could eat at the Oasis some nights."

"That's fine. The Oasis would be fine." It was my favorite place to eat, but I didn't want to act too eager.

"Well . . ." she said.

I also didn't want to be dismissed by some sort of queen

who ordered her subjects to come forward, then shooed them off, so I said, "I have to go now."

"Lydia?"

I turned back, careful not to be hopeful. She just wanted to ask me something else. Maybe she wanted me to go buy the lunch meat for supper. She didn't want *me*, I reminded myself.

"Yes, ma'am?"

"I thought maybe you might stay and have a snack with me. Oh, don't worry—I didn't cook one! I thought you might run over to the restaurant and get us a piece of pie."

I steeled myself. "No, I have to go now."

"Oh, well, some other time, then."

I opened the door and heard the horn blast. I thought it was saying, "Fo-ol! Fo-ol!" I wanted so much to stay. But I had to stop expecting her to be a mother to me. I had to close my heart to that, because it wasn't ever going to happen. Staying with her now would only hurt more in the long run.

Mother and I went back to the way we were before our fight. Not friends but not enemies, either. Dinnertime got a whole lot better. She began looking on the backs of canned goods for easy recipes. She found a tuna noodle casserole that wasn't bad. We also had baloney-and-cheese sandwiches— twice!

We had our best meals at the Oasis. I'd order a burger and fries, while Mother and Daddy ate something that I hated such as soup beans and corn bread. The best part of eating at the Oasis was seeing Elliot. He worked hard as a busboy, cleaning off tables, mopping up spills, and washing dishes. There he was, right out in the open, where I could watch him as much as I wanted. Even if we didn't exactly carry on a conversation, it made me feel better.

On Saturday night, while Daddy was paying the bill and Mother was in the ladies' room, Elliot came over to clean our table. He said, "Hey, Lydia." Just like old times.

"Hey, yourself."

He dropped a fork on the floor, I thought on purpose. When he leaned down to pick it up, he whispered in my ear. I leaned into him to hear what he was saying. He smelled like soap and his breath tickled my ear as he whispered. I straightened up and took a big gulp of air to clear my head.

"I'm sorry, what did you say?"

"I asked if you got one of Big Joe's special burgers with cigarette ashes on top."

"I must have. It was mighty tasty." I managed to get it out in a normal voice.

"I'll tell him how much you liked it."

We both laughed. It felt good to laugh with him again.

He got serious. "Willis told me how you've been reading to him. Thanks."

Before I could answer, Daddy came up and slapped Elliot on the back. "Hey, neighbor. How're things at the Merrills'?"

"Fine, sir."

"Good, good. Well, Ladybug, we need to scoot."

Mother returned at that moment and said hello to Elliot. I slowly stood. I wasn't ready to leave him or that warm feeling, but Daddy put one arm around me, the other around Mother, and walked us to the door.

I turned back and peeked over the top of Daddy's arm to

get one more look at Elliot. He was looking right at me, making a funny face and silently mouthing, "Ladybug?"

I laughed out loud, feeling better than I had since forever.

14

"You remember the rules, right?"

"Yeah," Willis said as he eyed the front of the library. He seemed awfully nervous. Well, the library always made me nervous, too.

I pulled open the heavy door. Cool air and the musty smell of old books blew into our faces. Willis looked at me and chuckled with excitement. I smiled, not because the library had *that* effect on me, but because I'd never seen him look really happy before.

We'd finally finished the raccoon book and Willis had told me he'd always wanted to hear the story of Tom Sawyer. I promised to check it out, but he insisted on coming, too. I wasn't at all anxious to have him and Mrs. Green in the same room, what with her thinking he was my boyfriend, but he wouldn't take no for an answer.

Inside the library, though, he got a wary look on his face. I looked over at the tall front desk with George Washington's picture hanging behind it. There was an American flag just off to the side. I guess it did look a little imposing. But, boy, if he was overwhelmed now, he should have been here before Mrs. Green ran the show.

I found *The Adventures of Tom Sawyer* soon enough. Willis reached for a book, then lowered his hand quickly. He looked around as if worried that he'd get into trouble.

"It's okay," I whispered. "Pick one and take a look at it."

He pulled a book off the shelf and reverently opened it. Then he looked at me with disgust on his face. "There ain't no pictures in here!"

"Well, no. Books for our age don't usually have pictures. We can get other books, though."

I took him to the little kids' section. He flipped through a couple of books and I think he would have liked them, but pride kept him from admitting it.

"These are for babies!"

"Yeah, they're for younger kids. But some of them are pretty good. I wouldn't mind checking out one for myself."

Willis snorted as if to say I was the biggest liar on the planet.

"Okay, if you don't want any of these, how about one like the book we had on raccoons? They've got photos in them."

He brightened up again. I was turning to the reference section, when who should I see standing there but Mrs. Green. I was scared she'd say something embarrassing, but she just gave me a big wink and went on replacing books on the shelf.

Willis decided on a book about insects, with lots of pictures. Then we went to the front desk.

Mrs. Green came over and said, "Good morning, Lydia!"

"Morning," I mumbled. This was the part I dreaded.

She held out her hand to Willis and said, "And good morning to you! I'm Mrs. Green."

She squeezed Willis's hand and he was too surprised to pull back.

"And what is your name, young man?"

"Willis."

"Oh! You must be Willis Merrill! I remember when you moved into town, and I'll bet you'll never guess how I remember such a thing."

"No, I guess not."

"I remember because I heard you had a pet raccoon and I said to myself, How interesting! How exotic! I've never had such an unusual pet. Now cats, oh, I have cats coming out my ears! And two dogs and a pet hamster in the summer. You see, my sister's a teacher and they keep a hamster in their classroom, but she travels in the summertime so I keep Recess for her. Recess is the hamster's name. They had a contest in her class and that's the name that won. Isn't that a cute name?"

"Uh, yes, Miz Green," I said, hoping she'd stop her yammering.

"Tell me, Willis, what is your raccoon's name?"

"Zorro."

"Zorro? How perfect! Oh, what a clever boy you are to name your masked pet after a masked crusader."

Willis actually seemed to stand a little straighter. He didn't smile, but his expression softened into one that didn't spell trouble.

"Listen to me rattle on! Now, which one of you is checking this book out?"

"I'm the only one with a library card, Miz Green," I said.

"Well! We can't have that!" She whisked the cover off her typewriter and sat down, rolling a card into the machine. "You both need library cards! Willis, tell me your address."

Willis's head shot toward me as if he wasn't sure what to do.

I mouthed the words "It's okay."

And for the second time since I'd known Willis, he looked really happy.

"So I get to keep this?"

"Yes, Willis," I said for the hundredth time. "It's your card. You can check books out of the library all by yourself."

"And they won't ask me if I can read 'em?"

"They don't care if you can read. They just care that you bring the books back two weeks later, okay?"

We were close to the Oasis when he said, "Can I stop at the restaurant and show Elliot?"

"You can show Elliot. You can show the Pope. You can even show President John F. Kennedy. I don't care!"

"No, I think I'll just show Elliot."

He said goodbye and shot into the Oasis. As much as I would have liked to see Elliot, I was glad for the break from Willis.

I walked home to get my bike. I didn't know where I was going, but I was feeling restless and wanted the wind to blow all thoughts out of my mind.

There are only so many roads you can travel in Maywood. After a while I ended up downtown and saw Mrs. Merrill and Beth come out of the Laundromat.

"Hey, Beth! Hey, Mrs. Merrill! Doing some laundry?"

"No, no laundry."

"Mama wrote lots of words and put them on the wall in here. Want to come see?" Beth pulled on my hand.

"Sure I do." I didn't know what she was talking about, but I wanted to be polite. I let Beth lead me inside.

Mrs. Merrill pushed her bangs off her face, looking flustered. "I just hung a little sign up to let folks know I'm doing hair now. At my house. While Boyd's at work. A little part-time job, you might say."

The sign gave directions to her house and said that the cost was whatever you wanted to pay. It also said Mrs. Merrill did hair only in the mornings.

"Wow! Ain't that something! And to think Nanna was your first customer."

Mrs. Merrill turned her face in that shy way she had.

"I didn't know you could get a beautician's license here in Maywood."

"Oh! You can't!" she said. "I'm not a real beautician at all. That's why I can't charge a set price. Without a license, I can only take what people offer me."

"I didn't know," I said.

"It's real important that you don't tell anyone I'm a beautician, Lydia. I'm just—" She stopped for a minute. "I'm just doing this on the quiet. To earn a little extra money."

"Well, I won't tell anyone about it," I said, wishing I hadn't said anything at all. Why was she doing it if it was such a big secret?

She seemed satisfied with my answer, though.

"Beth, come along," she said. "We have to get home."

I said goodbye and hopped back on my bike. I turned right

at the library and heard someone call my name, but I didn't see anybody. It was probably Bobby Wayans. He lived a block away.

"Is that you, Bobby?"

"Nah, it ain't nobody but me, Lydia. Look up."

I did, and there stood Willis on the roof of Esther's Dry Goods.

"Willis Merrill! What do you think you're doin'?"

"Come up and I'll show ya."

"How do I do that? There's no ladder that I can see."

From Main Street, the building was three stories high, but the roof stair-stepped to the second story. There was a room added on next to the alley, which was one story high. Willis was on the second story. He jumped to the first.

I yelled, "No!" thinking he'd break his danged neck, but he only jumped onto an upside-down burn barrel. Then he ran to the edge of the first story. Next to it was a telephone pole with metal spikes driven into the side for repairmen to climb. Willis took a leap from the building onto the pole and climbed as far down as the spikes allowed, then dropped to the ground.

He was so proud of himself, and I could tell he wanted me to be, too, but I said, "Do you realize how dangerous that is? You could have broken your neck."

"But I didn't. Come on!"

"I'm not climbing up there."

"Climbing up is the easy part."

"I *know* that. But I'd have to swing like an ape to get down!"

"What if I made it easier to get down?"

Sometimes I wondered why I'd taken on this project of giving Willis "special handling." Being around him was so tiring.

"How about you just tell me what it's like up there. And why you were up there to begin with."

But he had already moved down the alley. He came back with two old busted-up crates that he stacked next to the building. Then came an old tire that he propped on top of them. Together they reached almost to the first roof.

"There! You can climb up the pole, but when it's time to come down, you can swing over the side, land on the tire and climb down the crates."

"It looks awful rickety," I said, even as I parked my bike. Being bored can have a strange effect on you. It gradually seemed like an okay thing to do—till I got to the telephone pole, that is.

"The spikes are too high. I can't reach."

Willis suddenly grabbed me under the arms to lift me. "Ahh!" I yelled in surprise.

I lost my balance and my arms flew around in the air. I finally grabbed Willis's head. He couldn't see, so we staggered into the alley, where we both tumbled down.

"Dang it, Willis!" I lay there panting, but he was already up brushing himself off.

"Next time tell a person if you're going to grab them, for heaven's sake!"

He blinked and said, "Okay."

"You scared me to death, you know."

"Okay. You ready to climb up now?"

"Yeah. I guess."

"I'm gonna grab you now."

"Okay, okay. Sheesh."

This time I was ready and easily grabbed the spike. I climbed up the pole and jumped onto the first floor, with Willis right after me. He leaped onto the overturned burn barrel and reached a hand down for me. That's when I realized that I had yelled at him and this time he hadn't fought back.

Maybe being around him wasn't *all* that tiring.

We were on our stomachs looking over the edge of the building, which wasn't too comfortable, it being a tarred roof and all. I didn't complain, though, because Willis was enjoying it so much.

"Ain't it somethin' up here?"

"Yeah, it's pretty. You can see a lot of the town."

"Right below us is an apartment. See that door over there?" He pointed to what looked like a shed built right on top of the roof.

"What's the shed for?" I asked.

"Ain't no shed. You go through its door into the apartment. Wouldn't it be somethin' to live there? You could just walk out onto the roof whenever you pleased."

It made me nervous that we were on private property. "Maybe the folks who live here wouldn't like us being on their roof."

"Door's locked and they've never come out before. Probably aren't even home."

He rolled back over onto his stomach. "It feels safe up here—like nobody can hurt you."

"Like on your roof at home?"

"Yeah. How'd you know about that?"

"I saw you one night. I've been wondering about it ever since."

"Does your pa drink alcohol, Lydia?"

"Daddy? No."

"Elliot says it makes good men act bad. He says it makes bad men act crazy. Like I said, alone on a roof, nobody can hurt you."

It bothered me to think that Willis had a daddy who could hurt him.

Before I could say anything, he said, "Does this town have fireworks on the Fourth of July? 'Cause this'll be a great spot to watch them from."

"No, everybody goes to Aylesville. They have a parade and a little carnival. It's a lot of fun."

"Oh." He looked disappointed. "Well, forget that. Look yonder. I can see right over the library roof onto the Laundromat wall. I reckon I got the best seat in town for the Free Show. Hey, Lydia, you want to watch the movie up here with me next Friday?"

"Well, maybe for part of it. It is a good view, but don't you want to be with the other kids?"

He grunted and pointed to a gash on his arm. "So's I can get more of these? No thanks."

"Gee whiz, Willis! Did you get that when we fell just now?"

"Nah, ran into some boys. They was throwing rocks at me. That's why I was up here. It's my secret hiding place."

He grinned, but I didn't think it was funny. "That's awful. I didn't know the other kids were trying to hurt you."

"It's the same ol' thing. Happens everywhere we move. Being my friend is just fine till school starts. Once they find out I ain't all that smart, they don't want nothin' to do with me."

I sat up and picked little pebbles off the roof, tossing them to the ground below. "You talking about Bobby Wayans? He's not worth worrying about."

"Ain't just him. It's all them boys. Now that the school put me in Special Ed, they call me names, chase me and stuff."

"What kind of names?"

"Oh, you know, 'retard,' stuff like that."

A lump was building in my stomach. I tied my shoe to give me someplace to look other than at him. Before, I would have said he deserved it. Heck, I might even have cheered those boys on. And I'd called him a name, too—Ratboy. It hurt too much to think about that.

"You know, they probably wouldn't have put you in Special Ed if you had just told them you had trouble reading. If you'd been nice to the principal instead of spitting in his face, they might've just held you back in sixth grade next year."

"Ah, I don't think Special Ed is gonna be so bad. Nobody made fun of me. And the teacher? Mrs. Russell? She's right nice. She told me that my eyes don't see words like other folks' do. She said we'll work together, me and her, to get me readin'. She said I wasn't made like most people and that made me special. Hah! How about that?"

The lump was in my throat now, so I didn't answer him.

"The way I figure it," he went on, "those boys who poke fun at a person for being in Special Ed got it all wrong. They just think I'm different. They skip clear over the 'special' part."

15

I rode toward home thinking about what Willis's life was like. It made my chest feel tight. I wondered if that was how Elliot felt when he heard me making fun of Willis. No wonder Elliot had stopped being my friend.

I rode past Mother's newspaper shop. I needed to be around someone who would be nice to me. I turned at the post office, thinking I'd head back toward Daddy's gas station, when I realized I hadn't gotten the mail for the past three days.

When I pulled it out of the post office box, right there on top I saw an envelope with tiny, curlicue writing and knew right away it was from Nanna. I was so excited I tore it open in the post office.

June 28, 1962

Dear Lydia,

I was so glad to receive your letter. Meant to write you sooner but Louise talks all the time and there is always something keeping me from doing what I want.

As for the buttermilk cookies, am glad you like them but left all my recipes there. Had a feeling Evelyn would need them. Don't know if the recipe is in the tin or stuck in one of the cookbooks. Afraid I'm not much help but you can find it if you look.

Am glad Carolyn is doing well, although was worried when you wrote of her husband's arrest. I do wish you'd written more about it, as it alarmed me so.

Hope you are well, too, Lydia. I miss you and your parents. Louise talks more than the three of you put together. It's funny how you forget things over time. She always was a talker.

Goodbye for now,
Your Nanna

P.S. Am enclosing a note to Carolyn. Please see that she gets it. Also enclosed is your picture of Robert. Must have put it in my apron pocket that day. Keep it and don't feel like you're doing anything wrong by it. I gave it to you. It's yours. Love, N.

I'd give Nanna's note to Mrs. Merrill later. I was glad to have Robert's picture back. I'd wondered what had happened to it but was afraid to ask Mother or Daddy. And it made me happy to hear that Nanna was having a hard time getting used to her sister. Maybe she'd be back before Thanksgiving. I just wished she'd sent a batch of cookies.

When I walked out of the post office, I saw Willis heading toward home. I didn't know if it was because of our conversation on the roof or because of Nanna's letter, but I was glad to see him. I put the mail in my bike basket, and Willis pushed the bike as if he'd done it a thousand times.

"I got a letter from Nanna. Look what she sent me." I showed him Robert's picture. I hadn't told Rae Anne about Robert and I hadn't told Elliot. But here I was showing Willis.

"Looks like you."

"He's my brother."

"I didn't know you had a brother."

"Well, he's dead. He died before I was born, but he's still my brother. This picture is all I have of him."

"Then you'd best take care of it." I could tell by the way he said it that he knew it was important to me.

When we got close to home, I saw his dad's pickup parked at a crazy angle. It reminded me of that other time we'd seen him stagger across his front yard and Nanna had declared he was drunk.

Willis got quiet when he saw it. He probably would have run away if he hadn't been with me. I kept talking as if nothing was out of the ordinary and walked toward the backyard. If we could reach the tree house, maybe Willis would be able to avoid his daddy.

Suddenly we heard Mr. Merrill yell in a horrible, growling voice, "That's it! You're dead meat! I'm looking at some buzzard's supper tonight!"

"Oh no, Willis!" I said. "It's Zorro!" He was hanging on to the Merrills' screen door exactly the way he'd hung on to ours.

Willis reached the door just as it swung open and Mr. Merrill came out with a baseball bat. Zorro jumped off and Mr. Merrill was face-to-face with Willis.

"This is all your fault, boy! What have you got to say for yourself?"

Willis turned back into the old Willis. He stood there with that dead look on his face, saying nothing. It was as if he could leave his body and go to a different place when he was being threatened.

I inched toward the tree house and quietly climbed up. Mr. Merrill kept yelling words that didn't always make sense. He even shoved Willis a couple of times. But Willis kept his mouth shut. Finally Mr. Merrill threw the bat against the side of the house and yelled, "You can kiss that raccoon goodbye. If he ain't run off already, I'm gonna kill him next time I see him." He tore open the screen door and slammed it behind him.

Willis let out a deep breath and rubbed his stubbly hair with his hands.

"Psst! Willis!" I whispered.

He looked up and saw me. He was starting toward me when Zorro zipped past him and scurried to the tree house. Willis climbed up and grabbed Zorro. "Ain't he smart? He's about the smartest animal I ever seen."

"Yeah, he's smart. But what are you going to do now? I think your daddy will kill him. I really do."

Willis kept rubbing Zorro's fur as if he hadn't heard me.

"Now do you believe me that Zorro gets out of his cage by himself?"

I didn't think he was going to answer me, but he finally said, "That book. That one that told all about raccoons? It say anything 'bout turnin' them loose? You know, in the woods?"

Willis knew what it said. I'd read the whole book to him.

"They don't really know how to hunt for food or protect themselves because their owners have been doing that for them. It kind of kills their natural instinct. They have to be retaught and that takes time."

We sat that way for a while, just the two of us, staring out over Maywood's rooftops wondering how to save Zorro. And

Zorro sat nestled between us, probably thinking this was the best day of his life.

An idea came to me when I woke up the next morning. I threw on some clothes and hurried outside.

I rode to the library. Mrs. Green was walking up the steps to unlock the door when I yelled, "Miz Green! Wait! I need to talk to you!"

She jumped. It did my heart good to be the loud one for a change.

"My stars! You scared the daylights out of me. What is it, Lydia? Another overdue library book?" She winked when she said it. Even scared, she bounced right back to her old loud, teasing self—like a ball you couldn't keep underwater for long.

"No, Miz Green. This is personal."

"Ooh, personal. My favorite kind of talk," she said as she held the door open.

Her shoes clacked loudly as she strode across the floor. She threw her purse and lunch sack on the desk and said, "Whew! It's sticky already. Going to be another hot one, I'll bet."

I dropped my voice a notch, trying to get the conversation back to library level even though we were the only people there. "I have a big favor to ask. You know how much Willis Merrill loves his raccoon, right?"

"Of course I do! Do you need me to find another book on their care and feeding?"

"No, ma'am. What I need is for you to keep Zorro for him. You said how much you liked animals and how exotic you thought havin' a raccoon would be. Well, Willis can't keep him. It's a matter of life and death for Zorro. Willis needs somebody who'll take good care of him."

Her eyes went from normal to about twice their usual size.

"Goodness! I might have said those things but I was trying to—you know—make Willis feel good about his raccoon. It seemed to be his pride and joy, and I know how much you care for the boy."

"But you take your sister's hamster in the summer, right? And that's just 'cause she travels. Well, if someone doesn't take Zorro, he's gonna die. He'll either get murdered or die in the wild. Miz Green, please think about it."

"Oh, I don't know. Sam and I don't live in the country, you know. Is Zorro housebroken?"

I smiled at that. "No ma'am. He's not an inside animal. He stays outside in an old rabbit hutch. It wouldn't take up much room, and we could come by and help you take care of him."

Twenty long minutes later, I finally convinced Mrs. Green that we'd do all the work if she'd let us keep him at her place. Willis would be happy. That way he could still see Zorro.

"Don't bring him by before I get home. Sam will have a cow when he sees what I've done now!" But she was already piling all the books the library had about raccoons on her desk to read.

"One more thing. I know you're doing us a big favor, but Willis won't see it that way. He loves that coon so much, he'll think he's doing you the favor. Don't be hurt if he doesn't thank you."

Mrs. Green folded her arms across her chest and her mouth twitched as she said, "Is there anything *else*, Lydia?"

"No ma'am. Just this," and I gave her my biggest hug before I went to tell Willis.

16

As I pulled Mother's blue skirt out of the clothes basket and pinned it to the line, I thought of Willis. I hadn't seen him yesterday. It being the Fourth of July, Daddy, Mother, and I had gone to Aylesville to watch the parade and fireworks. But this morning, I could tell Willis wasn't the same without Zorro.

He had headed to Mrs. Green's house first thing to feed Zorro. Since he wanted Zorro to get used to his new surroundings, Willis planned to let him roam in her yard, calling him back if he went too far.

I reached for Daddy's shirt and looked across the fence at Mrs. Merrill. She had a customer in her backyard. She'd given the woman a haircut and was pinning her hair onto curlers. She'd had one or two people straggle in every morning since she put the sign in the Laundromat. She took them through her back door and washed their hair, but she always brought them outside to cut it. Maybe she didn't want the mess in her house. Or maybe she really didn't have much furniture, as Nanna had guessed, and didn't want anyone to know.

Holding Betsy in one hand, Beth was picking up the hair that had fallen to the ground.

I walked over to the fence and called out, "Hey, Beth! What ya doin' with all that hair?"

Just as she ran to show me, I heard wheels screech. I looked toward the street. Mr. Merrill slammed the truck to a stop in front of the house. I could tell he'd been drinking. Something wasn't right: he was never home in the morning. He almost fell out of the truck, then righted himself and slammed the truck door. He had a crazed look on his face.

Acting on instinct, I leaned over the fence and picked up Beth, then ran for my house with her in my arms. Whatever was going to happen, I didn't want her to see it.

At first she didn't say anything, but when we got to my back door her eyes were huge with surprise. I forced myself to laugh and swung her around so she'd think I was playing. I said, "Guess what? Your mama told me you could come play at my house today. I've got such big things planned for us!"

I set her down in the kitchen and took her hand.

"Come on. I'll show you where our bathroom is so you can wash your hands."

She looked down at her hands and asked, "Am I dirty?"

"No, silly! It's just that we're gonna have a big snack, so you need to wash them good."

She put Betsy and her collection of hair on the kitchen counter and went into the bathroom. While she was there, I ran back to the kitchen and looked out the window. Mr. Merrill was screaming at his wife. The woman whose hair she'd been doing was running down the street, dropping little pink curlers as she went. I opened the window a crack. Mr. Merrill grabbed the chair that the woman had been sitting in and flung it to the side. I heard him say, "What do you think you're doing? Did you think you could sneak around behind my back?"

Mrs. Merrill answered so low I couldn't make out her words. By then Beth was back, so I closed the window. I got out the Bugs Bunny cup I'd used when I was little and poured milk into it.

"What would you like to eat, Beth? We have cookies, or I could make peanut butter and jelly sandwiches. Which would you like?"

"Yes."

"Yes, what?"

"Yes, what you said."

"So you want both? Cookies and a sandwich?"

"Yes," and then, "Please!" She looked proud that she remembered to say please.

I placed the box of cookies in front of Beth and took the fixings for the sandwich to the window. Mr. Merrill was screaming louder. He said, "First I get fired! Then I come home to find you sneaking in a job! You know I won't allow any wife of mine to work!"

Mrs. Merrill ran inside the house and Mr. Merrill charged after her. I was sure he would hurt her.

My hands shook as I finished making the sandwich. I put it on a plate, threw a few cookies beside it, and grabbed Beth's milk cup.

The louder Mr. Merrill got, the more I worried that Beth would hear him.

"We're not having an ordinary snack, you know, so we're having it in a special place. Follow me!"

I led her upstairs to my room and opened my closet door.

When I was little, I loved to play in there. It was roomy and I had pretended it was my house. I pulled down a hatbox for a table and set Beth's food on it. Then I reached for my Ginny doll. I propped up Ginny at the box, put a cookie in front of her, and said, "Beth, I'd like you to meet Ginny. Ginny, this is my friend Beth. We're having a party!"

Beth clapped her hands together, then sat down very primly. If I hadn't been so anxious, I would have thought it was real sweet. Her forehead puckered and she said, "Lydia, Ginny doesn't have milk."

"Oh, you're right. And Betsy's downstairs. I think she'd like to come to the party, too, don't you?"

"Yes!" Beth clapped her hands again.

"I'll be right back."

I closed the door partway. I didn't want to scare Beth, but I didn't want her to come out and look over at her house. I made sure my bedroom windows were closed, then ran downstairs and out the back door.

Mr. Merrill was still yelling, and I thought I heard glass breaking. I didn't know what to do. I prayed that Willis wouldn't come home. I knew Elliot was at work and thought about calling him, but what could a fourteen-year-old kid do? He'd probably get hurt, too.

Then I heard Mrs. Merrill scream and I knew I had to do something.

I ran back into the kitchen and dialed O.

"Operator? Could you please get me the sheriff? It's an emergency."

I'd seen people call the sheriff on TV but never thought I'd have to do it. My hands were so sweaty I could barely hold on to the phone.

"Sheriff Yates here."

"Sheriff Yates? This is Lydia Carson."

"Lydia? Glen and Evelyn's girl?"

"Yessir, that's me."

"What can I do for you, hon?"

"Well, sir, maybe I shouldn't be bothering you, but our next-door neighbors are having a fight that sounds awful bad."

"Next door? You mean Boyd Merrill?"

"Yessir. Daddy and Mother are at work, and I didn't know what to do except call you."

"You did just fine, honey. But don't go over there. Stay inside your house no matter what happens, okay? I'll be right there."

"Thank you, Sheriff."

I must have been holding my breath because I felt I was letting it out for the first time since all this started. I finally got the phone back on the hook. I turned to the counter and tucked Betsy under one arm, then rooted around a kitchen drawer until I found two bottle caps to use as doll cups. I poured a dab of milk into each one and went back upstairs.

I played with Beth in that closet for what seemed like hours, although it was probably only a few minutes. When I heard the sheriff's siren, I closed the door and talked even louder.

I about jumped out of my skin when I heard Mother's frantic voice calling me. I opened the closet door just as she ran into my bedroom. She still had on her printer's apron.

"Mother?"

She stopped and threw her hand to her chest, trying to catch her breath.

"I heard the siren. One of my customers said it was coming from here and I just ran out of the shop."

My heart did a small leap until I realized she was probably after a story for her paper. She wasn't worried about me, I reminded myself.

"Is Lydia in trouble?"

I'd forgotten all about Beth.

"No, Beth. I'm not in trouble."

Mother got down on her knees and said, "Hello, Beth. I'm Lydia's mother." She looked into the closet. "What have we here? A tea party?"

"It's more like a milk party," Beth said, laughing.

"I wish I'd have known. Milk parties are my favorite kind," Mother said.

While they talked, I looked over at the Merrills'. Sheriff Yates was putting Mr. Merrill into the backseat of the police car. In handcuffs, yet! The sheriff said something to Mrs. Merrill. She was holding a rag to her face and shook her head. Then Sheriff Yates got into the car and pulled away.

"Mother? That, um, hair customer of Mrs. Merrill's just left."

"Oh! I'll go say hello to your mother, Beth. I'll see when she wants you to come home, okay?"

Mother came over and whispered to me, "Will you be all right?"

"I'm fine. It shook me up a little, though. When Mr. Merrill came home so mad and drunk, I grabbed Beth and tried to keep her from seeing it."

"Sounds like you did the right thing." She smiled at me.

"But Mother, I called Sheriff Yates. I'm not sure that was right."

"That's the hard part about growing up, Lydia. The right thing is rarely clear."

When Mother came back, we walked Beth home together. Mother whispered to me that she had cleaned up the broken glass.

Mrs. Merrill opened the door, holding a wet cloth to her swollen face. For Beth's sake I tried to find an excuse for her mother's appearance. A toothache, maybe? But Beth took one look at her mama and asked, "Did Boyd come home?"

Mrs. Merrill said, "Yes. But he's gone now. He won't be back for a long time."

Mother told me that Mr. Merrill might have gotten away with hitting Mrs. Merrill because she might have been afraid to press charges. But he'd made a big mistake. "He hit Sheriff Yates," she said. "You get into serious trouble when you attack a sheriff. Boyd Merrill won't be getting out of jail so easily this time."

I saw the basket of soggy clothes in the backyard and re-membered that I was hanging them when all this started. I was surprised when Mother began helping me. She clipped a dress onto the line, looked across at the Merrills' house, and let out a loud sigh. "I guess I'll never learn."

"Learn what?"

She pushed her hair out of her eyes and said, "That there's no such thing as a good drunk. You'd think I would have learned that from Philip." She shook her head and sat down on the porch step. I kept hanging clothes because I wasn't sure what I was supposed to do.

"After . . . after Robert died, you'd think I would hate all drunks, but no. When Nanna guessed that Boyd Merrill was an alcoholic, I just got angry. I think I was stuck in the habit of arguing with her. For years I'd tried to convince her that there was nothing wrong with a drink now and then. I defended Philip's drinking to her for so long that even after the accident, I never let myself blame him."

I stopped hanging clothes and sat down on the step below her. "I don't understand. Why would you blame your hus— I mean, Philip?"

"Because if he'd been sober, Robert might still be alive. Or maybe not. Who knows. At least Philip would have lived."

"But he died of a heart attack!"

"Who told you that?"

"Daddy."

"Dear Glen. Yes, he *would* try to cover for him. I guess it's time you knew the truth. Philip drank too much, but he was such a lovable drunk, never mean in any way. So I ignored it, reminding myself of all his good qualities. But the main reason I ignored the drinking was that I didn't want Nanna to know she'd been right about him. He wasn't 'good husband material,' as she liked to say. Oh, don't get me wrong—he loved me and he loved Robert. But he loved to drink more."

Mother put her head in her hands. I reached out to touch her, but stopped when she raised her head. The look in her eyes told me her thoughts were back in Ohio.

"When I realized that Robert had disobeyed me and gone fishing, I was angry with him. But I never really thought he was in danger. I called Philip at work and asked him to run by the lake on his way home to pick up Robert.

"I've relived that conversation a thousand times in my

head. I should have gone myself. I should have known that Philip had been drinking. Robert's friend, Alex, told me that he and Robert had been horsing around when the boat tipped. Robert couldn't swim back to the boat. Alex was trying to save him when Philip showed up. Philip jumped into the lake, but he'd had too much to drink. Alex had two people drowning, and he wasn't able to save either of them."

Mother looked at me. "It certainly wasn't Alex's fault. It was mine—and God's." She smiled weakly. "I guess we were both asleep on our watch."

"But, Mother, I don't see how it was your fault. You didn't know your husband was drinking—you said so yourself."

She stood up, took in a deep breath, and walked over to the clothes basket. She grabbed a shirt and hung it. Once again I'd ruined a good moment by opening my darned mouth.

We worked side by side until the clothes were hung. Mother picked up the empty clothes basket and stood still, holding it to her. A gentle breeze lifted the hair off her face. Her voice broke and tears welled in her eyes as she said, "It wasn't just the drinking, Lydia. Nanna was so *strict* with me as I was growing up. You know what she's like. I vowed that when I became a mother I would be more lenient. It was obviously a mistake. Maybe if I'd been tougher on Robert, he would have listened to me that day."

I laughed, and my hand flew to my mouth. It was such a wrong time to laugh. I was glad Willis wasn't there. He'd have boxed me for sure.

I reached out and touched Mother's arm. "I'm sorry! I'm not making fun of you, I promise. I was just thinking about all the Robert stories I heard from Nanna. Mother, do you really think anybody could have stopped him? I think Robert was Robert. The same way I'm me and you're you. I don't think anybody could have stopped him once he made up his mind to do something."

I took the clothes basket out of her hands and put it on the back porch.

"Do you know what I think Robert would say to you right now if he could? I think he'd say, 'I wanted to do it so I did it. I just never meant to make you cry.' "

But that's what Mother did. She slid to the ground and cried fifteen years' worth of tears.

17

Mother splashed cold water on her face at the kitchen sink. I handed her a towel and she smiled her thanks. "I've never felt so exhausted. I don't think I can go back to the shop."

"Would you like me to lock up for you?"

"That would be wonderful, if you're not too busy."

"No, ma'am. I'd be happy to."

"I'll call your father and ask him to bring something home for supper."

"I can do that, too."

She put her arm around me and said, "Thank you, honey, but I'd like to hear his voice."

On the walk to the newspaper shop, I thought the air had never smelled so fresh, and the sky had put on a new shade of blue I'd never before seen. Maybe it was because I was feeling something brand new. Some people call you honey so much you figure it's because they can't remember your name. Mother had put her arm around me and called me honey. With her, that meant something.

Daddy came home early that night. He handed me a sack from the Oasis, said "Hi," and took the stairs two at a time to check on Mother. I was opening the sack when they walked into the kitchen a few minutes later. Mother looked pale but seemed more relaxed than I'd ever seen her.

"Your mother says we had a bit of excitement in the neighborhood," Daddy said.

"Yessir."

"I'm proud of you, Ladybug. You kept your head about you."

I mumbled "Thank you" and kept on working, but his words made me feel good.

Mother said, "Lydia, I don't think I realized until today how much we've dumped on your shoulders."

"I'm okay."

"Oh, I know you've handled things beautifully. But I had a lot of time to think today, and that newspaper practically writes itself. I'm going to hire some help so that I don't have to do everything anymore. I also plan to close the shop a little earlier. At most I may have to go in one evening a week to fold the papers, but you two could help. It could be a little family job."

Daddy rubbed his hands together and said, "You're looking

at a former paperboy. I can fold those papers so fast you won't even see my hands move."

We laughed. Then Mother said, "I was wondering if you'd like to invite Rae Anne over for the weekend. Kind of give yourself a little break from all this housework and"—she waved her hand toward the Merrills'—"worry."

I thought about Rae Anne. Lord knows, I missed her. But then I thought about Willis. He'd be watching the Free Show on the roof of the dry goods store alone.

"No thanks, Mother. I've already got plans for Friday night."

Daddy got out dishes to set the table while Mother poured us drinks. With the three of us working together in the kitchen, I felt that this was the only place on the planet where I belonged. It was the nicest feeling, and I broke into an ear-to-ear grin that didn't change even when I realized Daddy had brought home soup beans and corn bread for all three of us.

On Friday night, Mother and Daddy got ready to go downtown early. We had all talked it over and agreed that we would buy a new automatic washing machine at Green's Appliances as long as we kept the old wringer washer hooked up and waiting for Nanna. It was easier to admit how much I hated that old wringer when Mother and Daddy were willing to listen to my fears about Nanna not coming back. They even discussed buying a clothes dryer, if it wasn't too expensive. Thinking about not having to mess with that clothesline made me almost light-headed with happiness. We laughed about how horrified Nanna would be by the expense. But as Daddy said, she might even like a clothes dryer during rainy spells.

Mother and Daddy left for the Free Show, but I stayed at home until it was time for Elliot to sell popcorn. I strolled along, planning to act as if I'd plumb forgot he had a job doing that. But he wasn't in front of the Oasis.

I went inside and didn't see him busing tables, either. So I waited until Hazel came to the counter to refill a customer's coffee.

"Hazel, is Elliot sick tonight?"

"Elliot quit, honey." She smacked her gum.

"Quit? Did he get another job?"

"Afraid you'll have to ask him that, sweetcakes." She pulled her pencil out from behind her ear and went to take another order.

Elliot wouldn't quit unless he had a better job to go to. That much I knew. It made me sad that I wouldn't be seeing him at the Oasis. I'd have to ask Willis where he worked now.

By then it was almost dark and I knew Willis would already be on the roof. I hadn't seen him since his daddy was arrested, and I just hoped he and Elliot didn't blame me.

I was almost at the alley when I noticed Bobby Wayans and two other boys looking at the pile of stuff Willis had made to help me climb down from the building.

One of the boys was Junior Plunkett. He grabbed the tire and started to heave it away, but the other kid stopped him. "Don't do that. Let's go up there and get him. Where's he gonna run to?"

They all laughed.

I tried to make my voice sound casual. "What's going on, guys?"

"Nothing that concerns you," Bobby said as he strutted toward me.

"Bobby, don't you have better sense than to talk to me that way? You know these boys won't be around you all the time and when they're not, you're plenty scared of me."

Junior jumped down between us. When school let out for the summer, we were about even in height. But Junior had grown since then.

"It doesn't matter how he feels when we're not around, because right now we *are* here."

I tried to laugh. "Junior, this doesn't have anything to do with you. You know me and Bobby always fuss when we're together."

"Yeah, I know that," he said. "I also know you've been hanging around that nutcase, Willis Merrill."

"Don't call him that!"

He shoved me and I took a step back. Junior had always been full of himself, but now he seemed downright mean.

"Yeah, give her a taste of her own medicine," Bobby called out.

"Stay out of this," Junior said to Bobby. Then he said to me, "What's wrong with you, anyway? Why are you nice to Willis? Are you retarded, too?"

Bigger than me or not, he wasn't going to get away with that. But then the other kid came up from behind and pushed me toward Junior. "Answer him," he said.

I landed on Junior's chest. Junior pushed me back to the other kid. This time he moved and I fell flat on my back in the alley.

Things happened real fast after that. I heard Bobby laugh when I fell, then squeal like a pig. I turned my head to look. Someone had jumped off the roof onto Junior. It was Willis. They were rolling in the alley, grunting and punching and ripping each other's shirts. I saw the other kid start over to help Junior. I had rolled to the side and threw myself against the kid's legs, knocking him down. He fell face first onto the gravel. I scrambled up and ran behind the telephone pole because I knew he could beat the tar out of me if he wanted. He raised his head, and his lip was bleeding pretty bad. He touched it with his hand and stared at the blood for a minute. He looked at Junior, shrugged, then walked away as if he didn't think the fight was worth the trouble.

Willis straddled Junior's chest. Both boys were panting. Willis said, "I ain't moving till you say sorry."

Junior said something I couldn't hear.

"Louder!" Willis said.

"Sorry!" Junior cried out. Willis slid off Junior and stood. Junior rose to his elbows and slowly stood up. Both boys' shirts were torn and there were splotches of blood everywhere.

Junior looked at Willis and finally nodded. I don't claim to understand boys and I don't know exactly what that nod meant, but I thought things were going to be okay between Junior and Willis from then on.

Junior limped away and Willis ran down the alley.

I thought, Gee whiz. Does he have to run every dang time something happens? But he came back in two seconds, pulling Bobby along with him.

"I'm sorry, I'm really sorry," Bobby blubbered. "I didn't want to hurt either one of you. Honest! It was those boys. They made me!"

"If it was them, then you'll be nice to us from now on, right?" Willis gave him another shake.

"Of course! I like Lydia. I like you, too, Willis. Honest."

I laughed. "Bobby, you are pathetic. Let him go, Willis."

Willis released his grip and we watched Bobby run away, looking back over his shoulder.

"You're a sight, you know that?" I said to Willis. He had a nasty cut on the side of his face.

"Yeah, I suppose I am."

The serial had already started and I didn't want to go all the way back home. "Come on, we'll run into Evan's Drugs and get some Band-Aids. That way we won't miss much of the movie."

He fell into step with me as we walked down Main Street.

"Willis, do you realize you showed those boys? That means they'll be nicer to you, don't you think?"

I could tell he was pleased but all he said was "Maybe."

"Still and all, you can't solve everything by hitting someone," I said.

Willis looked disgusted. "Didn't you just say I showed them? Weren't you soundin' happy about it? Now you're complainin'."

"I'm not complaining. I'm only trying to help you."

"Well, excuse me!" he said. "But I thought I just helped *you*."

"I didn't ask for your help," I said, but then I noticed Elliot coming toward us and words flew out of my head.

"Hey, Lydia," he said when we met up with him.

I gave out a weak "Hey."

He turned to Willis. "You need to get home and see Carolyn. She's got something she wants to talk to you about."

"Not now," Willis said. "We'll miss the movie. I'll talk to her later."

"No, this is important," Elliot said in that no-nonsense way he had. "You run on and I'll keep Lydia company."

My knees nearly buckled at that. I didn't exactly need company, but I wasn't about to tell Elliot that.

Willis hurried ahead of us. Elliot and I walked for a bit. He stopped and said, "How about we sit here and talk for a minute?"

We were standing by a house on a hill. There were three different sets of stairs leading to the yard. We were at the one farthest from the house. I sat down on a step and Elliot sat one below me so that our heads were about even.

I figured this was about his daddy. "I'm sorry I called the sheriff," I said.

"I'm not. If you hadn't, it's hard to tell what he would have done. What he *did* do was bad enough." He shifted on the step and said, "That's what I want to talk to you about. Carolyn and I agreed that things aren't going to get better. I don't know how much you've heard"—he looked uncomfortable—"but my pa is drunk nearly all the time. He— Well, this wasn't the first time he hit one of us, and that's just not right."

"No," I said. "Not right at all."

He looked at me. "He's in jail now. This may be our only chance."

"Chance for what?"

"Well, if we were to, say, go somewhere, he couldn't come after us."

I felt the earth shift for a minute. Did he mean they were going to leave? I'd just made friends with Willis. And little Beth—how could I not see her anymore? Then I looked at Elliot and thought about not seeing him ever again. If I'd been the crying type, I'd have done it right then and there.

"So you can see the spot we're in." He looked at me as if he really needed me to understand.

I cleared the lump from my throat. "Yeah."

Neither of us spoke. Finally I said, "But won't he come after you later? I mean, my daddy would track us till the end of time if we up and left."

Elliot snorted. "He'll look for a while, mostly because he wouldn't want anybody to think a woman got the best of him. The truth is, the only thing he'll really miss is his pickup truck."

We sat there for a minute. Without looking at me he said, "I don't want to leave. And if I could change one thing, I'd change the way I turned away from you. We had some good times until then, didn't we?"

"We did," I said. "But I don't blame you."

His eyes shot toward me in surprise.

"I was wrong about Willis," I said. "If I could change one thing, it would be the way I treated him."

He gave a little laugh. "I guess you would. When I wanted you to be nicer to him, I never dreamed you'd be his girl."

"His what?"

"I just never thought you might start liking him that way."

For once in my life I thought before opening my mouth. I thought about how I'd worked in the gardens, just so I could be by Elliot's side. I thought about how I'd quit riding my bike to school and going to Daddy's gas station just so I could walk home with Elliot. Up till that minute I thought I'd done it because I wanted a big brother. But something snapped in me when he said I was Willis's girl and, whatever that was, it made me realize how much I wanted to be Elliot's girl.

I turned to him and said in my calmest voice, "Elliot, you're an idiot."

I stood up from the step, dusted my bottom off, and walked toward home.

He called, "Lydia! Wait up!"

He caught up with me. "What did I do?"

"Just showed your stupidity, that's all." I kept walking.

He jumped in front of me. "Hold on."

I stepped around him and he grabbed my arm.

"I'm moving away," he said. "Can't you give me one minute?"

That did it. Saying he was leaving made me take a deep breath to ease the heaviness in my chest.

"Tell me what I did wrong. I don't even know."

"Let me give you a hint," I said. "If I liked a boy, I wouldn't act with him like I act with Willis. If I liked a boy, I'd probably work side by side with him in the hot sun, busting up dirt clods, just to be near him. Or maybe I'd walk home in the rain just so we could share an umbrella."

Elliot's eyes widened. "If you liked a boy, would you do something like offer to help him sell popcorn? Or maybe have *him* take a link out of your bike chain instead of your daddy who has a service garage for that kind of thing?"

"Yep, that's something I'd probably do."

He put his hands on his hips and took a deep breath. "Then I'm an idiot."

"I thought I already said that."

Neither of us spoke. Finally he said, "I don't have a job anymore."

"I know."

"I've always worked, so I never got to take a girl to the Free Show."

I swallowed hard. "I know that, too."

He smoothed back his hair, made sure his shirt was tucked in nice, and said, "Lydia Carson, I would be honored if you would go with me to see the Free Show."

I didn't say anything. I put my hand in his and we walked toward the grainy black-and-white picture that flickered on the Laundromat wall.

18

I sat in the tree house alone, watching the sun rise bit by bit. He wasn't coming. I'd been so sure he would. Suddenly his head popped up from the ladder.

I jumped and said, "You scared me to death! I thought you weren't coming."

"Why would you think a dumb thing like that?" Willis asked as he threw a sack onto the tree-house floor.

"Because we said sunrise. That was ten minutes ago."

"Maybe it comes up faster on your side of the fence," he said, smiling at his little joke.

He flopped down next to me, clearly excited. "Okay, I got everything I was supposed t'bring. How about you?"

"Yes." I handed him my sack.

He rummaged around, then looked at me. "I don't see no bandages."

"Bandages. Shoot! You're right. I forgot those."

"No bandages! You can't be trusted fer anything, you know that?"

I could feel my blood boiling, but I tried to keep my tone light. "Well, it's not like we're going to cut off an arm or something."

"You got that right. I'm not cuttin' anything now! No bandages," he muttered to himself. "You're worse than worthless."

I'd had enough. "Take that back."

"No." He looked as if he'd die before taking it back.

"Take it back, Willis, or I swear I'll call this off right now."

"Go ahead. Call it off. Who wants to be tied to you for eternity, anyways? I'm finding a new best friend. One I can count on. *He* won't forget the bandages!"

He climbed over the side of the tree house, leaving me there alone. I sat still. I heard something rustle.

"Willis?"

"What?"

"You coming back up?"

"Yeah, beanbrain. Don't know why, though."

He came back up the ladder and opened his bag. He took out an old metal lunch bucket he'd found at the junkyard.

"Won't that leak?"

"Might. I found a plastic tablecloth to wrap it in. *I* didn't forget anything."

"You're *so* funny," I said and handed him the scissors. "Don't cut off too much."

"Ah, tell your mom you got bubble gum in your hair. You got no imagination, you know that?"

I wasn't worried what my mother would think. I didn't want Elliot to see me with a big chunk of hair gone. All of a sudden, things like that mattered. But I just said, "You're right. That's what I'll tell my mom. About the bubble gum."

I felt the cold metal of the scissors against my head. One snip was all he took and I was relieved to see only a couple of dark curls in the lunchbox.

He handed me the scissors and sat down in front of me.

I ran my hand over his head. "I don't know what I'm supposed to cut. Your hair's so short your head is smooth as a potato. It's lumpy as one, too."

"That's all those brains of mine. Not enough room in one head for all my brains."

I laughed at that. He laughed, too. I sprinkled short pieces of his red hair on top of my darker strands. He pulled a pocketknife out of his back pocket and held it out to me. This was the part I dreaded.

"You go ahead," I said.

"Fine," he said. "I ain't no baby."

I couldn't stand to look. When I turned back, he had a trickle of blood coming out of his finger. He held it over the lunchbox.

"I don't think you're getting the drops on the hair," I said.

"Yes I am! Who thought this up, anyhow? You don't think I know how to make us blood brothers when it was my idea?"

I'd been letting the "brothers" part of this go. Willis came up with this as a way to say goodbye, and I was trying to do everything he wanted.

"Does it hurt?" I asked.

"Nah, no more than a sweat bee's sting."

I took a deep breath, bit my lip, and ran the knife edge over my finger. At first I didn't feel anything. Then a sharp pain shot up my finger.

"Sweat bee's sting my butt!" I said as I held my finger over the rusty lunch box, letting the blood drop onto our hair.

"Well, it might hurt a pansy like you."

"You're a riot this morning, Willis."

"Don't get your shorts in a knot. Take off your sock and wrap your finger in it till the bleeding stops."

"I'd never get the blood out," I muttered.

"It won't matter. Just throw the sock away."

"Good idea," I said.

"Who's gonna take care of you when you don't have me, Lydia?"

I peered into his face. He looked so serious. "I'll get by, Willis. I'll be okay." *We'll both be okay.*

He looked away quickly. "It's all done except for our most prized possessions. I'm putting in Zorro's collar."

Seeing it reminded me of the first time I saw that piece of rope—the day I met Willis. It was a good choice for the box.

I reached into my pocket and took out Robert's photo. I looked at his face for the last time, running my finger across the ragged part where Nanna had torn away his daddy. That picture had caused a lot of pain in our family, but it had also brought about healing. It was a good choice, too.

As I lay the picture inside the box, Willis said, "Lydia! You can't put your brother's picture in there! It's all you have of him."

"No, it's not." And I knew that to be true. "I have his hair. I have his eyes. And I have his mother. I don't need his picture anymore to know who he is." *Or who I am.*

I looked at Willis's worried face. "I'm gonna miss you, Willis."

"I know that."

We heard Elliot, down in our yard, clear his throat. "Willis? It's time to go."

Willis looked at me as if it had just hit him that this was really goodbye. He grabbed the lunchbox, quickly wrapped it in the tablecloth, and shoved it into my hands.

"You'll bury this right beneath this tree, right?"

"Right. And we'll meet here and dig it up ten years from today."

"Even if someone else is living here by then. And we'll never tell anyone."

"Blood brothers never tell," I said.

He climbed down first and ran to the front yard. I'd bury the lunchbox later. Elliot waited for me at the bottom of the tree.

He held out his hand. I slid mine into his. He gave me his sweet smile and my heart did a flip. It figured that we'd start liking each other as soon as he was leaving.

"I can't tell you where we're going," he said. "We can't take a chance on Pa finding us."

"I know."

"But later, after we get settled and Pa leaves here," he said, "I was thinking I might write you."

If I thought my heart flipped before, it was doing regular somersaults now.

"And I might write you back," I said.

He squeezed my hand and we walked that way, real slow, until we came around to the front of the house. Then we let go.

Mrs. Merrill was waiting behind the steering wheel of their truck with Beth tucked in beside her. Clothes were packed all around the little girl. Daddy was checking the ropes on the back of the truck, and Mother was talking to Mrs. Merrill. Elliot climbed over the furniture in the bed of the truck and sat down beside Willis and Zorro.

When Willis and I had asked for Zorro back yesterday, Mrs. Green had played it up just right. She said she had gotten attached to Zorro and wished he was hers to keep. She made me promise, in front of Willis, that I'd check out one library book every week in return for her giving him back.

Mrs. Merrill sat quietly, looking at their house.

Mother touched her hand. "This is for the best."

"When Boyd gets out of jail, you won't tell him where we've gone, will you?"

"Carolyn, please, we've been over this a hundred times," Mother said. "We'll tell him we have no idea where you've gone. It won't be hard to do, since you've never told us where you're going. It will be fine. Please don't worry."

But I knew I was the one Mrs. Merrill was worried about. I knew where she was going. That note Nanna had sent her had included a check made out to Mrs. Merrill for $250. Nanna told one of her white lies and wrote that she had won the money. She said there wasn't a thing in the world she needed but a good beautician. Nanna wanted Mrs. Merrill to go to beauty school in Louisville with that money.

I picked up the box that I'd packed last night for Beth. It had every doll dress I owned. As I passed it to Daddy to secure, I reached inside and pulled out my Ginny doll.

"Hey, Beth," I said. "I thought Betsy might be a little lonely at first in her new home. I thought she should take Ginny to keep her company."

Beth blinked her eyes a couple of times and looked real fast to her mama. Mrs. Merrill nodded. Beth turned back to me, then fought through the padding of clothes surrounding her until she got on her knees. She reached through the window and wrapped her arms around me. She whispered into my neck, "But won't *you* be lonely?"

I squeezed her tight. "Not for the dolls. Just for you."

There was one last flurry of goodbyes as Mrs. Merrill started the motor. Nanna would be so proud. She pulled that truck out onto the road just as smooth as a bird gliding across the open sky.

I waved until Elliot and Willis turned into a small dot and then vanished.

Mother put her arm around me. "Feeling sad?"

"Yes, ma'am." It was nice to lean on her after the weight of all those goodbyes.

Daddy put his arm around her and quietly said, "It's time to go."

She took a deep breath. "Yes. I'm ready."

We were having a memorial service for Robert. Daddy had had a small marker placed at the cemetery as a remembrance. Mother was finally getting to say goodbye.

She said, "I hope God doesn't faint when I show up in church."

"I think he can take it." Daddy winked at her.

She stooped to pick up a pot of yellow daylilies. She wanted to plant them by Robert's marker.

It was nice that she would have a place to remember Robert. We climbed into the car and it suddenly dawned on me that I wouldn't know which marker was his. "Mother? No one's ever told me Robert's last name!"

"It's Emerson," she said. "Robert Emerson. No middle name."

My head jerked up at that and I'm sure I stopped breathing.

"I couldn't think of a middle name I liked. Then someone I loved and respected said to me, 'When that baby is born, look into his eyes. If he looks like he has character, he won't need a string of names to tell the world who he is.'

"When I looked into Robert's eyes, I just knew he would be someone the world would have to reckon with." She turned to me and said, "I felt the same thing when I looked into yours."

Tears rolled down my face. I wondered why I had ever hated crying. I'd never felt so good in all my life.

"Who—" My voice broke and I tried again. "Who was the person you loved and respected? The person who helped you decide not to give us middle names?"

"It was Nanna."

"But you and Nanna fought all the time!"

"I know, honey." She sighed. "Relationships can be so muddled and confusing. You'll see what I mean when you're older."

Daddy pulled the car onto the road and I rolled down my window. As the sun shone on my smiling face, I thought, I don't need to wait at all to know that.

Author's Note

As I wrote this story, I wanted Willis to have an unusual pet. Since Willis is a little untame himself, I thought a raccoon would make a great one. But wild animals really don't make good pets.

Raccoons are intelligent creatures, and very curious. They are great at climbing, swimming, and running. While they aren't normally aggressive, if cornered they can fight fiercely enough to kill a dog. Raccoons often carry diseases that can be harmful to humans, especially to children.

Most states have regulations concerning ownership of raccoons and other wild animals. In my state of Indiana, a permit from the Division of Fish and Wildlife is required to keep a pet raccoon, which needs special housing.

If you ever come across an abandoned raccoon, leave it undisturbed and contact a licensed rehabilitator, who will care for it, teach it how to survive, and then release it. Your state's fish and wildlife agency can direct you to a licensed rehabilitator.

Acknowledgments

In writing this book, I was fortunate to have the help of a terrific writer's group. Thank you, John J. Bonk, Lisa Williams Kline, Lee P. Sauer, and Manya Tessler. Thanks, too, to Laura Backes for her wonderful suggestions.

I was especially lucky to catch the interest of my discerning agent, Steven Chudney, who did a superb job of matching me with my editor, Beverly Reingold. I am truly thankful to both of them. I'd also like to thank Lisa Greenwald, editorial assistant, the second person at Farrar, Straus and Giroux to care about my little story, and Beata Szpura, for the terrific jacket art.

In researching the Linotype machine mentioned in the story, I spent a most enjoyable afternoon with Mr. Cecil Krebs, editor-publisher of *The Boswell Enterprise* (Indiana). I'm so glad I got to see his "working museum." Thank you, Mr. Krebs.

Kathy Jones, Carla Lincicum, Linda Keller, Jane Woodworth, Richard Lincicum, and Jerry Keller provided input in recreating this era and/or gave enthusiastic support during the writing of this story, and I appreciate their help so much.

Last, but never least, special thanks to my family—Mark, Cam, and Catie—for their love and encouragement, and for putting up with me all those months in which I walked around with my head stuck in 1962 in a small Indiana town.